the
thir
sto

KT Finegan

Betty Books

Published in 2016 by Betty Books

Copyright © 2016 KT Finegan

KT Finegan has asserted her right to be identified
as the author of this Work in accordance with the
Copyright, Designs and Patents Act 1988

ISBN Paperback: 978-0-9955000-0-6
ebook: 978-0-9955000-1-3

Published with the help of Indie Authors World

IndieAuthors
World

This book proved to me that dreams come true, so don't worry about how to make them happen. Leave that to a higher power, instead spend your time doing what you love, and let go of the worrying. Miracles happen in magical ways that we can never expect. So I dedicate this book to the dreamer within us all. Don't stop dreaming

Acknowledgements

my thanks to the MacLeod family for all of your faith, guidance and support, and special thanks to the magical editing of Christine McPherson. Thank you. To my family; my sister Elizabeth, thanks for putting up with me, niece Eli and nephew Oli, you are both my stars. Mum, Dad, and baby brothers Billy and Garry. We'll meet again, I know that. Ian, what can I say apart from 'every step of the way' Cailean, another star. And to all my friends, those who have been with me forever, those I knew only for a while, and those I've yet to meet. Thank you for everything. And especially to the girls- Alice, Angela C, Angela M, Anne, Bernadette, Eileen B, Eileen R, Fiona, Frances, Grace, Hazel, Jen, Mairi, Mary, Mattie, Michelle, Shirley, Stephanie, Suzy, Wilma. Thanks to all of you for sharing my soul story, for your support, your encouragement and your friendship. And finally to my wonderful English teachers at Lochend Secondary School- Mr Mcleod and Mrs Irvine. Thank you for supporting a little girl who liked to write, this is the culmination of that. To all teachers out there, never underestimate your impact on the children you teach.

Foreword

We are delighted to have KT Finegan as the winner of the first Calum Macleod Memorial Publishing Prize (2015).

We sadly lost our son Calum to meningitis in October 2007. It was this tragedy that fuelled Sinclair's desire to follow his passion for writing and led to him self-publishing his own crime fiction books. Our business - Indie Authors World, developed to help other writers follow their dreams and it seemed a fitting tribute to create a fundraising publishing prize to celebrate what would have been our son Calum's 21st birthday. We had many wonderful entries which helped raise over £700 for the charity Meningitis Now.

The judges had a tough job choosing a winner but we all agreed that Karin's emotive writing hooked us. We all wanted to know more about Kirsty and the mysterious thirteen stones. What had Kirsty's beloved Grandmother's death unleashed?

We were thrilled when we got to read the rest of the book. It is a great story on many levels with interesting characters and mysterious developments as Kirsty explores her family's heritage and connection to the stones.

We hope that you will enjoy the book too and we wish Karin lots of success as she steps into her passion for writing.

Calum made such a difference to many people's lives while he was on earth and we are so proud that his legacy is continuing to make a difference. If you want to know more about this year's publishing prize please visit our website – www.indieauthorsworld.com.

With love and gratitude,

Kim and Sinclair Macleod

1

Calloused hands had long ago carved Rest in Peace on most of the grey, moss-covered gravestones scattered across the old graveyard. It overlooked Lanark the small Scottish market town I called home, and I felt it was a constant reminder of their own mortality to the people who lived there. Along the old greying sandstone walls, pale pigeons and dark crows watched our procession as we walked in black clothes, shoes, hats and handbags. Silently, and moving slowly behind the coffin carried by the black-suited undertakers. No male relatives or friends were left to offer their strength, either emotional or physical, on this sad day, so it fell to strong-shouldered strangers to bear our burden. One of the birds sang a long, slow song of the dead and forgotten, and I shivered, cold in my body and with frozen feet and fingers.

The pain in my heart since hearing of the death of my grandmother had now spread to my head. My temples and behind my eyes burned and ached from shed and still unshed tears. As I looked around the graveyard, the pressure from the grey sky hanging only inches above my head added to my tension and feeling of claustrophobia. Here, at the highest point of the town, with the big expanse of sky, and the mountains in the distance, the wind ripped through my lightweight black jacket, right into my core. I doubted that I'd ever feel warm again.

We stopped at a newly-hacked hole in the ground, right at the centre of the graveyard. Around us, old stones lay on their sides, broken angels and crosses scattered in the dust, mixed up and weathered so badly there was no way of knowing where they had started. This was the oldest part of the graveyard, and where the blacksmiths, the bootmakers, the apothecaries, the weavers, and the stonemasons were buried. Long dead trades marked in looped script on old grave- stones for long dead souls.

Unlike the rest of the cemetery, these graves were unkempt; no flowers, no little solar-celled lamps, no plastic-coloured windmills, and no gold paint on shiny black marble. Stones here were from earlier centuries when the town thrived and some could afford to mark the passing of their loved ones in granite tombs. Names no longer in fashion, like Euphemia and Thomasina, in illegible etchings on ten foot high memorials barely hanging from the stone and flint walls surrounding the graveyard. Some graves were marked only by small stones or crosses, the names erased by time and weather. Others standing tall but broken, names, dates and loved ones faded away.

I felt my eyes fill again with frozen tears, my sight blurred, pain in my heart, and tight sobs escaping from my throat, even though I was trying to hold onto my grief. I knew that my grandmother had purchased a plot beside her mother's grave a long time ago, but until this moment its purpose hadn't really sunk in. All those visits to this place in brilliant sunshine with flowers cut from our garden, watching Granny tidying gravestones, picking up weeds and throwing away dead flowers. It hadn't really meant much to me.

I had no feelings for those stones because that's all they were to me. They were names from long before I was born. Not real people; people who cared for me, who loved me, fed me and hugged me. People who telephoned and wrote long letters with all the local gossip when I moved away. The thought that I'd never again hear my grandmother's voice pierced my heart like a dagger of ice, and I gulped back the solid sadness in my throat.

I realised with a shock that the Minister had stopped talking, and was looking at me. I felt a flutter like a wing on my arm and a whisper in my ear from the smallest, teeniest little lady there. 'A very old and dear friend' was how she had introduced herself this morning at the undertakers. 'Kirsty, dear… it's time.'

I lifted heavy eyes and noticed that the Minister was offering some earth to me. No part of my body wanted to take it, but I didn't have the words to try to explain this to any of these people. Instead, my fingers found some soil and I realised with a fright that the coffin was now at rest, nestled deep down in the earth. *How did that get there?*

As I'd stood with head bent low, the undertakers had done their job, silently releasing the ropes and sliding the satin wood down into the ground. There was a putrid, dank odour in my nose and my stomach churned. In church for the earlier service, I hadn't dared look at the coffin. It felt so final. Knowing my flesh and blood, my beloved granny lay within it, was too much.

I added a little white rosebud I had snapped from one of the wreaths, and sent it down with all my love and longing for this beautiful woman who had given so much to me. I heard the Minister say Granny's name… 'Kirsten Cairngeal Wallace… ashes… dust'. I was tuning in and out, and felt myself focus on the undertaker standing a short distance away. Anything to keep calm and in control when I wanted to scream and shout and cry, but not in front of all these people, strangers to me. I felt I had to hold on to show Granny I could be strong. For her.

The undertakers were a small family-owned business, and had 'taken care of the arrangements' for the loved and unloved of this little town for a very long time. I remembered James Jack from school, and even then he had known he'd be an undertaker one day. I always thought it weird to have a family business like that. I should have realised that this was the nature of this town, and I was soon to find out that we had a 'family business' as well. One that I could never have imagined. But now it was Granny's turn to be 'arranged', and the pain in my heart and throat threatened to completely overwhelm me.

Yet even then, part of me felt removed from all of this as if I was watching it through water or some sort of emotional filter. I don't think I had caught up with the other me who had taken the phone call, booked the train from London, talked to the Minister, the undertaker, the solicitor. Actually, thank God for them all, I thought, and thank God that Granny had already made the arrangements in advance. She had known that her time would come, and didn't want to leave the burden to me. All I had to do was arrive, and I'd managed that.

Since that phone call last Wednesday morning to say that Granny had slipped away in her sleep, nothing was very clear. I had arranged time off work; the government department I worked for had been much more accommodating than I had expected. And as hard as it was to think about it, since I'd been dumped by Derek a month ago, I didn't have to consider anyone else. The next thought crashing through, and the one I'd been holding back so that I didn't sink further into self-pity, was that Granny's death meant I didn't have a single living relative in the whole world.

I couldn't remember my grandfather. He had died before I was born. Old photos showed a kind and handsome face. My father had died when I was a baby, my mother when I was ten. Both of them had been only children. No brothers, sisters, cousins, aunties or uncles. I had never felt so alone, so completely and helplessly and frighteningly alone. It threatened to overwhelm me, so I bit it back, and pushed it deep within.

Even with that, though, something was bothering me about all this; some niggling doubt, a memory deep in my brain, some little idea that had been trying to work its way through my shock, my grief, my tears. Something didn't feel right. Granny had been in perfect health. Even for a 75-year-old. And as far as I was aware, she had no intention of 'passing on', as she always insisted on calling death. Granny always said she was here for a reason, and by that she actually meant 'here'. In this quiet little town, sitting in the very middle of Scotland. Or Alba, as Granny had always called it, the old name for Scotland meaning the land of the light.

I had no idea why this was all so important to her, but I knew that it was. I knew it went beyond patriotism, love of her country. It was love of the country, the land, every river, hill, blade of grass. She had a passion so great for everything to do with this land that she had never left it. Not once in all her years had she left this place. Every night she slept in the house she had been born in, not one night or day away from this town. I could never imagine what that must have been like. So many times I had tried to entice her to come down to London or take a holiday somewhere else. But she wouldn't leave.

At that moment, standing on that windy hillside overlooking the town and countryside so loved by the woman we were now burying, I could hear her voice in my head. It gave some comfort in a way. As I breathed deeply and felt the tears falling onto my cheeks, I could remember the feel of her arms around my shoulders. It was as though she stood just behind me, and for a moment I was sure I could even smell her soapy smell.

What would she have said to me if she was here? I tried to concentrate on that; the feeling of her in my heart. I blocked out everything else, sounds, smells, the people all around me.

I focused on my heart, and tried to slow down my breathing. I felt something different. Something softer, something beyond my pain. It was love, pure blessed love. She would have told me that everything happens for a reason, she would have said she loved me. With that thought, the tears flowed freely down my face, but I felt more peaceful. I had a sense that death wasn't going to get in the way of how we felt about each other, and that helped me feel a little better.

I rubbed my tired eyes with my gloved fingers as cold splatters of rain – never far away in this part of the world – hit my head, and the grey sky darkened further and lowered down, settling almost onto our shoulders. I saw the concerned look on the faces of the other mourners. Old friends and neighbours, all elderly, and all looking very frail. Most rarely ventured out during the day, never mind after dark, and I was touched that they had come out for the burial.

With a quick nod from the Minister, we walked back down towards the road, past the old sandstone chapel to St Kentigern, roofless, windowless and leaning dangerously to one side. Past the old stone crypts and broken walls that had separated the very rich from the rest of the town, even in death.

Finally we reached the cars waiting to take us all to the local pub for some food. It wasn't a far walk, but Granny had arranged transport with her elderly friends in mind.

I didn't look back as we walked away from the grave. I didn't see the council workers move in to fill in the earth around the coffin. I didn't see the flowers and wreaths placed on top of the grave. And I didn't see the wind hit and separate a bundle of bones, skin and feathers; all that remained of the beautiful songbird.

2

We arrived into the welcome heart of The Three Keys at the top of the Wellgate on the main road through town. It took a little time to help some of the ladies from the cars and show them into the lounge area, but it was everything anyone would want in a local pub. It had real log fires in the winter, sold all sorts of real ales, and real food was on the menu. It had been in the same family for years. I remembered a time of stolen kisses in the playground with Billy McGuire, and holding hands when no-one was looking. He knew he'd run the pub when he grew up. The town was that kind of place, continuity was important, and the big supermarkets were yet to find a way in to take over trade and close down businesses. The locals were continually raising petitions and the local newspaper regularly raised concerns, but most of the shops were still independently proud.

I was exhausted; none of the other mourners ate much and said very little. I had a feeling that Granny's death had shocked them as much as it did me. We all had a hot drink, and there was lentil soup, sandwiches, sausage rolls, and scones with butter, double cream and jam – a traditional Scottish funeral fayre. The McGuires always catered for the town's funerals and they had arranged the little wood-panelled lounge in tables set for four. Floral china milk and sugar bowls and small teapots with spouts that dribbled tea every-where but into the cups.

Nothing warmed me up. Nothing could reach the ice block inside me, not even the kindness and warm wishes from Gran-ny's friends. None of the ladies drank alcohol, and as much as I could really have done with a very large glass of wine I resisted. As soon as the last of the ladies had left, I thanked the waitresses and asked for the bill. An older-looking Billy from the boy I remembered came over to shake my hand, give his condolences, and tell me that they wouldn't accept any money.

'Kirsty,' he said, 'your granny was everyone's granny in this town. She helped us all and there is no way I am taking a penny from you. I am so sorry that she has gone, it won't be the same without her. Please take care of yourself, and if there's anything you need just let me know. You're not on your own, you know. We all feel the same.'

His thoughtfulness started fresh tears and I almost ran out of the bar after whispering my thanks. I wasn't used to being so emotional; I rarely cried. I didn't want to break down in front of him, but his kindness and obvious respect for Granny was overwhelming. I realised how much she had done for the people of the town, with her advice, lotions and potions. A fresh wave of loss overwhelmed me and I had to rush for the door. I wanted to feel cool air on my face and in my throat and lungs.

The pub was in one of the older parts of this very ancient town. It was said that there had been a pub on the site for over four hundred years. The thin higgledy pavements were so narrow that two people could not walk side by side with-out stepping onto the road. And the cobblestones, although quaint to tourists, meant walking in high heels was difficult.

I heard the church bells count out five o'clock, and it was already dark outside with the wet weather and the short daylight hours of late November. I pushed my way through the early Friday night drinkers who struggled to get in past the smokers filling the pavement outside, trying to avoid splashes from the buses and cars passing inches away on the shiny cobblestones.

Lost in painful thoughts, struggling to hold back tears, perhaps I wasn't really paying attention to where I stepped, but I gasped as I felt a hand on my back pushing me hard. As I twisted round, I lost my balance. I saw dazzling headlights, heard brakes screeching, people shouting, and I felt myself falling into the blinding light. There was no way I could stop myself. I closed my eyes. My body tensed for the inevitable. Expecting pain. Blackness. Time slowed. Stopped. I saw Granny smiling at me. Arms out to reach me. I felt her love. I heard her say my name.

3

I waited for the impact. Instead, I felt a strong safe hand at my arm, lifting me back onto the pavement. The bus trundled past, the driver cursing me. I was standing outside the pub with everyone looking at me, and recognised the friendly brown eyes of Billy, who must have followed me out. The look of horror on his face showed how close I'd been to danger.

'Thanks, Billy. I don't know what happened there.'

'Jesus, Kirsty! Are you ok? I don't know what happened either, but I thought you were about to fall under that bus! How did you manage to keep your balance?'

With those words I realised that he hadn't touched me; he hadn't been close enough. It must have been someone else. What other explanation could there be, after all?

'Did you see who helped me, Billy?'

'I didn't see anyone, Kirsty. Look, these things can happen. Come back in and sit for a while. I haven't opened the lounge back up yet. It's nice and quiet. Let me get you a brandy to settle yourself. It's been a hell of a day for you.'

'No thanks, really, you've been great today but I'll head back. It's been a long day. Thanks again for everything. I just want to get to bed now.'

I had booked into Rosebank Guest House only a couple of minutes away, in one of the row of sandstone cottages not far from the graveyard and the train station. It was a pretty white house, similarly styled to the rest of the town. Rendered and painted sandstone, with two bay windows on either side of the centred front door and porch, two dormer windows in the low, sloping, red tiled roof, and cheerful yellow paint on the windows and door. I really couldn't face staying at Granny's cottage on my own, with the funeral and everything.

But as I left the light and sound of the pub behind me, I shivered, whether with cold or fright I did not know or care. For the first time ever, I was conscious of the dark and the quiet all around me. The muffled sounds of a train leaving the station came to me across the darkness and I realised that fog had settled silently over the town. It became thicker as I walked, isolating me from landmarks and the usual lights and sounds I'd known all my life. I had never seen such a thick fog and was worried as I walked because I couldn't see more than a few feet in front of me.

One or two cars passed me with their fog lights on, but their orange glow failed to illuminate the darkness. I knew to keep the barbed wire fence of the railway line to my left hand side, but wasn't sure where to leave it and cross over a small road to reach the entrance to the B&B. My breath quickened, and for the first time ever I was scared about walking around my town. I had walked that road so many times, with friends and on my own, from school, shops, train, bus, the pub. Never once in all that time had I been worried.

You know that feeling you get when someone is watching you? I had it. The feeling that someone or something was close. That it could see me. That it was coming closer and I couldn't see it. An invisible predator in the thick fog. I was alone, walking as quickly as I could with pinched toes in high heels. My frozen feet slapped against the pavement and I felt dread in my stomach. My body tight with tension, my hair damp with sweat at the nape of my neck. I sensed rather than heard a strange noise behind me. Like an animal breathing and moving softly, hunting its prey. Me.

A car slowly passed me in the gloom, and I felt whatever was behind me pull back a little. At the same time I felt my toes kick small stones and gravel and I realised that there was a wooden slat fence on my left hand side. The B&B was close by. I speeded up, determined to get inside, through the gate, and down the gravel path to the porch. I still couldn't see a thing but I heard heavy breathing like an animal coming from in front of me. It had changed direction. I wasn't going to reach safety. It was going to catch me and I had nowhere to run.

4

T he breathing came faster and was upon me before my brain had caught up with the situation. I let out a gasp as a little bundle of white dog jumped at my knee.

'Kirsty… Are you all right, pet? We were getting worried about you so I thought me and Bertie would walk round to find you. We never get fog as bad as this. I thought you'd be frozen so I brought your coat with me. Bertie, get down, down! Sorry, Kirsty, but he looks really pleased to see you.'

Relieved, I almost leapt into her arms. 'Mrs Thomson! Thank you so much. I feel really stupid, but I was getting scared and thought I was lost. And I thought something was following me. So stupid really. Thank you. Thank you.'

Mrs Thomson, the B&B owner, fussed around her little west highland terrier, trying to untangle his lead from around my legs and hers, leaving me time to recover my composure. It must have been the sounds of the dog sniffing around that I had heard through the fog. Whatever else could it have been, after all?

It was so kind of her to bring my coat, and I snuggled into its quilted down and felt better as we walked for a few minutes to reach the porch, Bertie leading the way. He was such an excitable friendly wee dog, and my favourite breed.

Mrs Thomson opened the door of the B&B, and as she took Bertie's lead off he rushed around the hallway rubbing his body across the panelling and seeking out toys. The place smelled of furniture polish and the morning's toast… and now wet dog. The hall was full of shining furniture, with bright yellow rugs on the dark floorboards. It was quaint and clean, and very homely. Everything felt light and safe after my experience walking back from the pub.

I headed down the hall to my bright room in the modern extension at the back of the property. It was painted pale lemon, with bright floral curtains at the window, matching bedding, and another yellow rug on top of the blue carpet. Not really my style, but very cheerful. It smelled of lavender air freshener and furniture polish, and reminded me of Gran's house. As I closed the curtains from the dark foggy night, Bertie ran after me with a squeaking soft toy and I was glad of the distraction.

Mrs Thomson followed him into the room. 'He's always full of fun, so he is. I know you've had a hard day, Kirsty. It's difficult to say goodbye to the ones we love, and you're so young to have lost so many… Do you want Bertie to stay and play with you for a while? He really is a tonic when I'm feeling down. I've been a widow for five years now and I don't know what I would have done without him. I really feel he got me through it.'

I immediately agreed. 'If you're sure you don't mind, that would be great. I'd planned to have a bath and early bed, but… could he stay with me in here?'

'We can try, pet.' She smiled gently. 'He might stay, but be warned he'll want to be in bed beside you. He likes his luxury, does that one I've got him spoilt, I know, but he is so loving. Maybe you could let him be with you for a wee while and then send him out when you want to sleep? He'll find his way back to my rooms when he feels like it.'

We both laughed as Bertie reappeared with more toys, as if he knew we were going to have a play date. So while I ran a bath in the en-suite, he ran about after toys and we had a quick tug-of-war with an old thick rope. After a few minutes he collapsed with a deep sigh in the corner of the room, as if he was exhausted. The fun had changed my mood and I found myself in a better place than I'd been all day.

I left Bertie in the bedroom and undressed and stretched out in the hot water, hoping it would warm me up. But as I lay back in the bubbles, breathing in the steam, exhaustion and a deep longing suddenly overwhelmed me. It was a physical pain in my heart and sobs stuck in my chest. I was too tired and emotionally drained for tears. This was so raw, so painful, so much more hurt than I could ever remember.

Although I suppose I must have been upset when my parents died, I really couldn't remember much about them, or how difficult it must have been for me or Granny after their deaths. It was such a very long time ago, and I hadn't thought about them, especially my mum, for years. After she'd gone, Granny and I used to look through photographs, and lots were dotted around the cottage. So maybe, over the years, those images became my memories. I couldn't remember the person, the voice, or the touch of her, only that of Granny who became my mother and father.

I couldn't settle in the bath, and pulled myself out with what felt like the last of my energy. Drying quickly, I wrapped my hair in a towel and fell into bed. I automatically lay on the left side, as I had done every night for three years with Derek. With another deep sigh and some defiance, I fidgeted across and forced myself to lie down in the middle of the bed. Tears of self-pity forced themselves from under my lashes.

Why was life so hard? What had I done to deserve all this? What do they say: 'what doesn't kill you makes you stronger'? Rubbish!

I was exhausted, and so very tired of crying. When Derek and I finished, I had thought that was the worst that could happen. My trust, my love, my life had been in the couple that

I thought we were. Although I accepted our relationship was over, a little part of me would have given anything to have him with me at that moment. Someone to cuddle into, to hold and be held; that's what I missed. The last few weeks had been full of tears and pain, and the same thoughts going over and over in my mind. The routine of work was the only thing that had kept me going; everything else was different, destroyed.

Bertie seemed to sense my need for comfort and I felt him jump onto the bed and snuggle down beside me. As I lay in the darkness, sniffing back more tears, the whole crazy story reran in my head for about the millionth time. Derek's late nights in the office and his business trips, but even then I hadn't been suspicious. Then I found a receipt from a jeweller's in his suit pocket when I took it to the cleaners. Thinking he had finally bought a ring, I had expected a wedding proposal for my birthday. I planned how surprised I'd look when I opened the box, spending sleepless nights wondering about what it would be like to be married to him. Except that when he handed me my present, I opened up a fleece onesie, comfortable and sexless to wear sitting in front of the telly, and a box of Maltesers instead. They're not even my favourite chocolate.

I thought I'd made a mistake, maybe he'd propose later. I decided to surprise him at the office one night when he was working late. There they were, him and his secretary. Not working. All such a cliché, and all the more painful for that reason. I was devastated and so humiliated that I didn't want to tell anyone at first, until I realised that I would need somewhere else to stay. We lived in his flat.

I remembered what Granny had said when I'd told her I was moving in with him. She had asked if it was wise to give up my own place. She probably knew it wouldn't last but she didn't push it or try to get me to change my mind. She wasn't like that. She was always very intuitive; she just seemed to know things. Lots of people came to her for guidance.

Thankfully, my best friend Susie had a spare room, and didn't hesitate to offer it when I said I was leaving Derek. So many times we had discussed someone else's break-up over tea and home-made scones. We both loved to bake our way through heartbreaks, so there had been a lot of cakes in the years we'd known each other.

My own words had come back to haunt me: 'no-one leaves a happy relationship.' And even though it was painful, in my heart I knew that I hadn't been happy with Derek for a long time. I'd hoped for happiness, wanting things to change but not knowing what to do.

By the time he got back that night, I had packed all my clothes and some personal stuff into a couple of large suitcases and left them in the middle of the hall, so that he'd see them as soon as he opened the door. Not very mature, but I suppose I was hoping for a reaction that told me he loved me and we could sort things out. Instead, he told me he was relieved that I knew, and had been planning to finish with me anyway.

Pure Scottish bravado got me through that. A great show when my heart was breaking, but I held back the tears until I handed back the keys to his flat.

I hadn't told Granny. I was too ashamed, and had been working up to breaking the news. How stupid. And now I wouldn't be able to be comforted by her, because I know that's what she would have done. Instead, I'd avoided telling her because my stupid pride had got in the way.

I cried then for the loss, for me and for her. I heard and felt Bertie snuffling around and licking my fingers as if he understood my pain.

In the strange bed, sleep eventually came but my dreams were full of images of graves, and dead birds, and falling down holes, to deep caverns in the earth. Fighting my way back up again and then falling down again. Feeling that I'd woken up and was safe, and then the image of falling again and knowing I was still in the middle of a nightmare. I could hear someone, maybe a woman, calling my name over and over: 'Kirsty, help me! Kirsty, help me!' I woke up a couple of times in the night with a terrible feeling that something awful was going to happen, then I remembered that Granny had died, and the grief of loss would come again.

I drifted in and out of sleep, sometimes lying awake hearing the church clock chiming, feeling the bed uncomfortable beneath me. Wrinkled sheets and lumps and bumps in the bed pushed against my skin. All my life I'd suffered from disturbed sleep, bad dreams, sleepwalking. I sensed the dog shift, and his breathing brought me comfort. I wasn't alone.

Somewhere in the quietest, darkest part of the night, I woke again with a fright and the awful sensation that someone or something else was in the room with me. I lay still, too scared to move, as terrified as I had ever been in my life. Hardly breathing, I lay in the dark, listening, all senses alert with a feeling so intense only the primeval part of my brain could cope. I dared not move.

I thought I could hear breathing. Deep, heavy breathing, like an animal, a large animal, somewhere in the room. I knew it wasn't Bertie. I kept my eyes closed, and felt somewhere in my mind that this was like a memory. It had happened before, in another bedroom a long time ago. Or was that a memory of a long forgotten nightmare? But this was real. I was awake. I was terrified.

Scared to take a breath in case whatever was out there in the darkened bedroom came closer, I felt Bertie tense against me. He started to growl.

I sent up a silent prayer to God, to Granny, to anyone who loved me to help me. I was scared for me, and for Bertie. Suddenly the words of the Lord's Prayer came to mind, softly edging their way into my thoughts. 'Our Father who is in Heaven, Hallowed be thy name…' The prayer filled my head.

I felt Bertie relax again, and the next thing I knew I woke up as daylight lit the room, and I let the dog out to join his mistress. I snuggled back under the duvet and dozed off again until the sound of the church bells striking ten woke me.

$\overline{\underline{5}}$

Despite the heat from the big bulky radiators in the room, I shuddered at the memory of the previous night. It must have been a nightmare. After all, how could there have been someone or something in the bedroom? I must have been more stressed than I realised, as that's usually when I'd experienced nightmares in the past. The dog had probably reacted to my tension, nothing else.

It had been a horrible day and my imagination had been playing tricks on me. I had tripped at the pub, not been pushed. Someone had helped me although I didn't see them, and there was nothing odd about the fog and no-one there apart from Mrs Thomson and her amazing dog Bertie.

I got up quickly, showered, and took tea from the tray in the room, as I had missed breakfast and didn't want to put Mrs Thomson to any bother. I didn't have any appetite anyway. Misery surrounded me like a thick blanket and my head ached. I dressed and left the B&B.

Something was calling me back to the graveyard, some feeling that I should go back. I felt I wasn't at peace with Granny. I should have told her what had been happening. Regret burned in my head.

The early morning was dull, the sun was missing from the northern winter sky. Although the fog had cleared considerably, there were still wisps of it around and I couldn't see the mountains any more. I walked back along the narrow pavement, the ancient walls of the two-storey buildings tilting towards each other and almost meeting above my head, making the day seem darker.

Claustrophobia added to my tension and I was relieved to see more of the grey sky on show as I crossed the road and entered the rusting cemetery gates. My feet scrunched on the red-chipped pathway as I walked uphill, past the derelict chapel and the remains of an old crypt. I could see a little white butterfly dip up and down, flying low and serene in this sad place. Then I realised it had to be a moth, after all it was November and Scotland.

I shuddered as I walked past the decapitated body of what must have been a pigeon, feathers scattered over a grave like a burst pillow.

Must be lots of happy cats here, I thought. And I stopped. Someone was bending over my grandmother's grave. A long-haired, slender woman crying; I could hear her sobs. She fixed some flowers then brushed some imagined dust away from the freshly packed soil on top of the grave.

I stood for a moment, unsure whether to intrude on this private grief. This was someone who cared deeply for Granny. As I looked closer I had to blink my tired eyes as she seemed to shimmer in the light. It was like looking at a hologram hovering in the air; one minute I could see her clearly, the next she had shifted out of focus and looked like coloured dust sitting in the air in the shape of a person.

The woman, or whatever she was, seemed to sense that she was being watched and turned round towards me. I could feel the blood drain from my head as the face looking back at me was the image of my grandmother, but a younger version. *Or an older version of me*, was the thought that flashed across my brain.

The woman hesitated, and then asked, 'Kirsty?' Or at least that's what I heard in my head. I wasn't sure if she had moved her mouth or spoken out loud.

'How do you know me? Who are you?'

She slowly pushed her long, light hair back from her face, in a gesture that looked familiar. We appeared to move closer together, or so it felt, and now I could clearly see her bright green eyes. She transformed from translucent to colour and back again. By this time I wasn't sure if any of this was real or not. I knew Granny had believed in spirits. But I didn't. I really didn't. This wasn't real. It was a trick of the light and imagination, and grief and tiredness… and guilt.

'Oh Kirsty,' I heard somewhere in my head. 'It's me. Mum. It's been a very long time.'

There was a scream or shout, as if from a long way off, a deep roaring in my ears, and a dizzying fall towards blackness.

6

I was aware of cold chilling dampness in my knees and hands. The metallic taste of blood was in my mouth, a sharp pain in my head and ribs. Feeling lost and diso-rientated, I slowly opened my eyes, wincing as the pale light hit me. I had fallen sideways and a large, ~~stone,~~ angel headstone had broken my fall. Otherwise I would have hit the sharp stones which covered this part of the graveyard.

Luckily for me I had managed to stay almost upright as I passed out, striking my mouth, head, and ribs against the stone. Very tentatively, as my whole body ached, I pulled myself upright. I wasn't badly hurt but I was very confused and felt a little dizzy. I didn't know how long I'd been unconscious but I was chilled to the bone.

The shock and surprise hit me as I glanced over at the graveside. The whole graveyard was empty apart from the big black birds sitting along the top of the abandoned chapel.

What had that all been about? Was she really my mother? Did I see a ghost? No, impossible.

There had to be another explanation. I could hear people talking from over the wall to my left hand side, and within a few moments a man and woman walking a big black Labrador came towards me. They asked if I was okay, and I assured them I was fine.

When I asked if they had passed anyone else on the path-way, they both shook their heads. I must have looked a fright.

It was kind of them to be so concerned, and the woman looked back a couple of times as they walked on. But I didn't want to talk to strangers. *What would I have said?* They would have thought me crazy. No, this was just because of my grief. My mind was playing tricks on me. It had to be.

I found a broken piece of masonry and sat down gingerly, my head swimming again. In my mind I could picture long-buried images of my mother, conversations with my grandmother, images and sounds of a family life, but all from a very long time ago. Memories, I was sure. More than those old photographs had ever given me. I could hear her voice, I was sure of it. Images of us laughing and dancing around the cottage. Sunny days, picnics, reading in bed under the covers with a torch. Lots of pictures came to me, fast, one after another like someone had speeded up a video recording of my life.

After my mother's death I had gone off to boarding school in Edinburgh. I think Granny wanted to make sure I was okay and got a good education, but I hated it. Home had been for the holidays only. It took me ages to make friends at school and I learned quickly that no-one likes a cry baby.

I thought so much of my childhood had been forgotten. But was it ever? Recently, the nightmares had felt so real that I'd begun to wonder if there were some memories mixed up and wanting to come out for a visit. But the sensible administrator in me, and the dull accountant in Derek, hadn't wanted to believe that could be the case.

Whatever had just happened to me must have been some sort of waking nightmare. *Could such a thing exist?* The 'woman' had gone, apparition or imagination. I felt drained.

Stupid fool, I told myself. *She died years ago, and you haven't thought of her in a long, long time. You're tired, and upset. Now, it's time to get a grip. People will think you are mad.*

Even though Granny had believed in spirits, it had always seemed so silly to me, and totally unbelievable. I shivered as I walked away, and at that moment I missed the presence of my gran even more, if that was possible. She would have loved to have had this discussion with me.

I thought of all the times over the years that Granny had tried to talk to me about 'her work'. I liked to think of her as a herbalist, making up creams and lotions in her kitchen for local people, as her mother had done before her, and hers before that. I suppose I knew somewhere deep down that she did a little more than that, but I had never ever wanted to talk about it. I had always wanted to be practical, and believe in science and reason, not spirit and faith.

Slowly, limping slightly, I pulled on a pair of black suede gloves I found in my pocket, then headed out of the graveyard and back along Station Road. Some things about the town were exactly as I remembered them, but other things had changed. There was a new school up behind the graveyard, built deep into what used to be a hilly area. They builders must have taken a way a lot of earth, as the ground floor was so low down I couldn't see it fully from the roadside.

I spotted the bright lights of a new retail park on the other side of the road, built on the site of what used to be the livestock market. Around the fencing someone had tacked up a hand-painted banner protesting about a new extension to the quarry on the other side of the graveyard. I noticed some council workers stop to take it down and throw it into the back of their van.

As I walked along I probed around my mouth with my tongue for damage, but apart from a sensitive raised area at the back of my lip, I was okay, at least physically. I walked along towards the High Street, and past the black and gold painted railings of the imposing Church of St Mary's.

Set back from the road in an immaculately tended court-yard, it was over three hundred years old and had recently undergone a multi-million pound renovation. Last time I had been in town, the building wore a shroud of plastic sheeting around its skeleton of scaffolding.

Its vastness surprised me. For the first time ever, I saw the church in its full majestic glory, and I realised why people came from all over the world to see it. It was already floodlit, the day as dark as night, and the newly-cleaned granite sparkled under the lights. The church stood easily three storeys high, and longer than two football pitches. High, arch-shaped, multi-coloured stained glass windows glinted from the lights inside.

There was something so grand and beautiful about the place. It was breathtaking and, despite the sharp winter's air, I stopped at the gate. We were so high here that the church seemed to sit on the clouds like something from a fairytale. The stained glass windows were designed by a famous artist, and the middle window caught my attention. With the lights from inside the church I could see the pattern on the glass. I'd always thought it was something like St George and the dragon, like the story. Although, I suppose why that would be here in the middle of Scotland and in a church called St Mary's escaped me.

Standing looking at the window, I realised that it was a woman, not a knight, standing in front of the fire-breathing dragon. She was holding up a ball of some kind, like an orb but one that shone with a pale blue light all around it like a halo. The image, now that it was cleaned up and lit from behind, was really clear. She was tiny against the size of the dragon. Dressed as in medieval times, her long blond hair was in a braid down her back, almost to her belted waist. Her face showed compassion; love even, not fear. And around her head was a golden halo as well.

I could see that the dragon had half turned, as if looking behind him to a large doorway, and the background looked like they were in a cave. It was an odd scene, but one of bravery, especially when she was unarmed in front of the dragon. The vibrant colours sparkled in the light.

The churchyard was landscaped with little white sandstone cobbled blocks, and under the floodlights these shone and looked magical. Right in the middle of the courtyard was a simple wooden cross, perhaps twenty feet high. As I looked, the lights for this flicked on and the cross seemed to shimmer in the light.

I'd never been very religious and it was a long time since I'd gone into the church, but I immediately felt it was a very beautiful, welcoming place. The word sanctuary came into my mind for some obscure reason. A blackboard at the gate announced that a guided tour was about to start – something new for the town.

While I stood there, a busload of Spanish tourists descended, all trying to get in the narrow gates at the same time. Not wanting to share the experience with so many people, I decided to leave a visit for another time. I had no idea it would be so soon and under such strange circumstances.

$\overline{\underline{7}}$

next to the church stood what used to be an old gatehouse, set against the stone wall surrounding the rest of the church grounds. It was now a coffee shop, with a glass conservatory added to the front. The steamy windows looked inviting, and I had to smile at the name emblazoned in lilac fluorescent lights across the front of the café: *Angel's Cakes*. What a great name for a place so close to the church.

I pushed open the door, and walked across a darkly varnished wooden floor. Immediately the sounds of chat and laughter hit me, along with the sweet aroma of cakes baking in an oven and freshly ground coffee. Some of the old stone walls were exposed, with flickering candle-effect lighting and big circular black chandeliers hanging from the ceiling on chains.

There were about half a dozen wooden tables and what looked like old church pews as seats to the left of the room. Straight in front of me was a big wooden counter, a glass-fronted fridge filled with cakes – lots and lots of cakes – and the reassuring hiss of a cappuccino machine. A couple of older women were paying their bill at the counter and chatting away happily, so rather than crowd them I moved over and almost gasped out loud in amazement.

The whole right hand side of the space was set out like a shop. Dark wood shelves displayed hundreds and hundreds of angels. Every kind of angel. Glass, wood, cloth, plastic, wax. Statues. Candles. Lights. Toys. Teddy bears with angel wings. Pictures. Wall hangings. Books. Cards. CDs. Every surface, shelf and wall was full of angels, in every colour, size and type. The effect was mesmerising.

As a child I had been an avid collector of all things angelic, but I had forgotten all about it until the effects of this crazy, unexpected little space hit me. I felt I could breathe here and let out a deep long held sigh. I felt my tension ooze away like mist in the air, as if an angelic cloud surrounded me.

As I wandered around the shop, picking things up, squeezing stuffed toys, softy touching the faces of the angels of stone and wood, I was entranced. And a feeling of peace overcame me. I had found a little haven amongst all my pain. I knew my gran would have loved this.

I was aware of some music playing behind the chatter and clatter of the coffee shop. Beautiful, almost angelic female voices singing. The tone was hypnotic in a way, and I relaxed a little more. The smell of the coffee signalled a rumble in my tummy, and I realised how thirsty and hungry I was, as I hadn't had breakfast or eaten much over the last few days. That was unusual for me, especially when I was stressed.

Back at the counter, a fair-haired woman was smiling, waiting for my order. 'You must be Kirsty,' she said. 'I knew your grandmother really well, and I knew you'd pop in when it was the right time. Are you okay? '

I didn't have a clue what to say to that, and if I hadn't been looking into blue eyes with a cheeky glint from behind thick spectacles, I would have been upset. Instead, for the first time in what felt like ages, I smiled back at the woman. She looked a little older than me, maybe in her fifties; it was hard to tell. Her blond hair was pulled back away from her face and she wore a black apron with *Angel's Cakes* in purple swirly script across the chest pocket. She was so friendly and attentive.

I ordered a large latte, some soup, and a big slice of carrot cake. All of the cakes looked delicious and were obviously home-baked, hence the wonderful aroma of baking. The woman told me to take a seat and she'd bring it all over.

I headed towards a recently vacated leather sofa looking out onto the street, and shrugged off my coat, scarf, and gloves. A few minutes later a steaming mug of coffee was in front of me, and the soup quickly followed.

I stifled a giggle when I saw that the mug had an angel on it, as did the napkin wrapped round the cutlery. Served with loads of creamy butter on thickly sliced brown bread, the soup was delicious and warmed me all the way down to my toes.

Feeling a hundred times better, I looked around and sipped at my coffee whilst waiting for the cake. I had the distinct feeling that someone was watching me, and as I turned my gaze back to the counter, I saw the lady who had taken the order talking with a taller, older woman. She was very smartly dressed in a mossy green tweed skirt suit, with a cape of muted rust orange brown and green over one shoulder. I wasn't sure of her age, perhaps sixties or early seventies.

It was obvious that they were discussing me, which would normally annoy me. But in the circumstances, the whole town probably had something to say so I decided to let it go and try not to brood on it. Looking round the empty tables, I realised that I was the only customer left.

Stupid fool, I chided myself. *They probably want to clear up and get home, that's what they were saying.*

The fair-haired woman arrived at my table with a huge slab of carrot cake, and another steamy latte.

'Are you trying to close up?' I asked. 'I'm sorry, I don't want to hold you back.'

'Not at all, there's no hurry. Take all the time you need. I'll be here for ages yet, cleaning up. We were just saying how much we missed your grandmother and how you look like her. There's a strong family resemblance.'

I looked into those bright blue eyes, already filling with tears to match my own.

'I'm Angel,' she said.

How appropriate, I thought. *Another angel.*

I realised that I couldn't speak about Gran. The words wouldn't come and I didn't know if I'd cry, and I didn't want to start in case I couldn't stop. It was easier to change the subject, so I cleared my throat a couple of times before trusting my voice not to shake and give away my sorrow.

'I love your angels,' I told her. 'When I was younger I loved them, but it's been a long time since I really thought about that. I felt so good when I walked around and saw you had so many angelic things for sale. And that music is beautiful. It made me feel more relaxed… I didn't know you could buy so much. I suppose being right beside the church you get lots of religious people in?'

I had forgotten about the childhood magic you can enjoy with a toy, or how the simplest things can take on great importance. For me it had been angels and unicorns. I'd loved them, and had lots of toys and little ornaments and statues. I wondered what had happened to them. I hadn't taken them with me to school, or onwards to university or my adult life in London. I guessed Gran had probably cleared them away years ago, and I felt a little tremor of guilt on how quickly I had dropped my childhood comforters.

'We get lots of people who are welcoming angels back into their lives. People who used to believe in fairies and magic, but felt they had to leave that all behind as adults. So there's something really special about seeing people reconnect with that childhood innocence and sense of fun,' the woman explained kindly. 'It's not all what you would call "religious people" we get in here. Some people just love angels, and like to come in and browse. I love their energies. I also have crystals and meditation stools and cushions, Himalayan salt lamps, bowls. You name it, I probably have it!' She laughed.

'I really thought angels were only for children.'

Angel didn't seem to take any offence at my words. Instead she laughed again, and I felt an immediate closeness, which was very unusual for me.

'I suppose I was the same,' she admitted. 'I loved angels and cherubs when I was younger as well. I remember I had a magical unicorn toy and I could tell that toy anything. The fashion then was to swap paper scraps, and my favourites were all the angels. It sounds so simple now, not like kids today with their technology, but my friends and I would spend our pocket money on all different pages of little images that we could cut out individually and place in a book.

'If we wanted to swap a particular image, we would pull that one out of the top of our books, and our friends would look through to see if they wanted to swap for one of theirs. It was all the rage with the girls. The boys swapped football cards, the girls swapped scraps. And then, I suppose a bit like you, I sort of forgot about that and grew up. I went to Glasgow and trained as a nurse and then worked in the local hospital and got married.'

My eyebrows must have risen slightly, and she seemed to know what my question would be without me voicing it.

'No. I'm not married now. I got divorced about five years ago and that's when I got back into my love of angels. You could say meeting my Guardian Angel saved my life.'

What could I say to that? I didn't want to be rude, and she seemed sincere but also a little eccentric in her rainbow-coloured top and brightly coloured glasses. Maybe I was just too used to dark business coloured clothes, and I realised I was wearing black trousers, top and coat. Even my bag, scarf and gloves were black, which was my normal attire, and not bought especially for the funeral or sad times. This darkness had become my life.

My sceptical side must have been apparent to her, as she carried on speaking.

'Honestly. I know it probably sounds crazy to you, and if anyone had told me that before I met my angel I would have had them carted off to a mental home. But I met my Guardian Angel and my life changed for the better. And I love my life now. Don't get me wrong, it's not perfect, but I don't believe that's what life is about. And I know that it is perfect for me. I know I can get through the sad times and I know I always have the love and support of the angels. It makes life so much easier. I don't have to worry about anything. I turn problems over to my angels and things work out without me fretting and making myself ill the way I used to do when I was nursing.'

The woman sat down on the other end of the couch before carrying on. 'Look at me now. I'm making a living doing what I love to do. I meet wonderful people. I have fun. I might not have a big house or fancy car, but I realised that I don't need anything like that. And it's all down to meeting my Guardian Angel. Can I tell you what happened?'

I nodded. I was desperate to know. It's not every day you meet someone so content and with an inner glow, doing what they love. I realised that was what the glint in her eye was – fun, joy, happiness, confidence, contentment. All the things that I realised I wanted in my life, but were sorely missing.

'If I go back to when I was nursing, I was so stressed. I was unhappy and unfulfilled, but I didn't know what to do about it. I suppose I kept myself really busy so that I didn't have to look at how I felt about my life. And although I was married, I didn't have any fun in that either. We didn't have any children, not because we didn't want them, we just didn't seem to make time and then it was too late for me. All my friends had got pregnant and were raising children, and it didn't happen for me.'

Her smile faded a little and for a few moments, she looked sad. 'We didn't talk about it. In fact, we didn't talk about anything that mattered. I felt I was on a hamster wheel: I got up, went to work, stress, stress, stress, I shopped, cooked, ate, watched telly, and went to bed. There didn't seem to be much fun in my life. It was as if Malcolm and I were going through the motions. We hardly spoke to each other, and when we did it was about things that had happened to us, always about outside events, if you know what I mean.

'I suppose I put it down to the fact that we were both working long hours, he was an ambulance driver, so often our shifts meant that we didn't see each other for days at a time. He liked to work night shifts as there was more money in that, and it took me a long time to realise that in a way I preferred when he wasn't there. It was as if we shared a house but not our lives. Does that make sense?'

It was as if she had just described my life with Derek. Like she was ahead of me in some way. I knew exactly what she meant. 'So how did angels come into your life?' I asked, desperate for her to continue.

Her happy smile returned. 'Now that's an amazing story. I really wasn't happy with my life at that time, but I couldn't have told you why or made any effort to change things, because I didn't know how, or even that I had a choice.

'I was approaching fifty and I realised that I was over half-way through my life and felt it hadn't started yet. My mum and dad both died within a couple of months of each other, and that knocked me for six, I can tell you. Nothing prepares you as an adult for becoming an orphan. It seems silly, and I know you've had tragedy in your life, but I felt I was adrift on an ocean. Malcolm hardly mentioned their passing, and that's when I realised that nothing was going to change unless I made some changes.

'I was so hurt by the way he carried on as normal, without acknowledging how my life had changed. I had been so close to my dad especially, and I missed both of them all the time.

Anyway,' she paused briefly, while I waited anxiously to hear her story. 'I decided to make some changes by going to a diet club, and started a yoga class. To me, yoga sounded posh and for rich people with lots of time on their hands; I was terrified that they'd look down on me and that I wouldn't fit in. But I decided I had to test myself and get out of the comfort zone, so rather than watch the soaps two nights a week I signed up for yoga at the sports centre. That's where I met my Guardian Angel.'

'What? At a yoga class?' I squealed.

Angel laughed. 'Well, you know at the end of the yoga class when you lie on the floor and they do a wee bit of relaxation?'

'I'm not really into yoga, but I think I know what you mean.'

'My yoga teacher had all sorts of symbols around the room. I didn't really understand what they were, but every week she would talk about the energy in our bodies. At first it was lost on me. I couldn't even pronounce half of the words she used and I didn't like to ask anything. I was so self conscious and scared of saying or doing the wrong thing. Gradually I learned over a few weeks that yoga was about balancing our energy centres, called chakras. The teacher explained that was the word for wheel in Sanskrit, which is an ancient language used in India. We each have a wheel of energy at different parts of our bodies, even under our feet, at points along our spine, and above our heads.

'Each of these chakras has a specific colour, symbol, and sound, and can be brought into balance and when they do we feel better. It was exactly what I needed to hear, the idea that I could be helped into balance. It sounded so good, and I really enjoyed our after-class relaxation time. Our teacher called it yoga nidra and said twenty minutes was equivalent to four hours of good sleep. Well, as you can imagine, I hadn't been sleeping well. I was still grieving for Mum and Dad, and I knew that Malcolm and I were going nowhere –to be honest, we were heading in different directions.

'He didn't want to talk about anything and couldn't seem to help me. I was drowning, adrift somewhere in my mind without a lifebelt. It was as if every day I sank lower and lower. I'm not one for going to the doctor's for myself, and maybe that's where I could have gone. Instead I was at a yoga class.

'So.' She sat a little straighter on the couch, and I found I couldn't take my eyes off her as she spoke. 'That particular week the teacher started to talk about angels. I kid you not, I was lying flat on my back with my eyes closed and she said that angels are all around us, and that if we gave them permission they would come close. I remember thinking, "Please, please, please, come to me!"'

'Oh my gosh! What happened?' I was enthralled by her story. It was impossible not to be.

'As I said, I was lying there, on my yoga mat on the floor of the church hall, when I felt a light come into my head. That's the only way to describe it. Like someone switched on the light. I got this strange feeling in my heart, like a sensation, a pulse, a strong feeling. I didn't know what it was, but I started to cry. Tears poured from my eyes and I was so glad that we were all lying there in the semi darkness. It was a feeling of light so hard to describe, but I knew that something was there.

'Then a voice in my head said, "I'm here for you." I knew it was my Guardian Angel. I dried my eyes and got up and out of the hall as quickly as I could, and headed home. But guess who I bumped into right outside the hall?'

'I don't know… your angel?' I whispered.

She laughed again, and this time there were tears in her eyes when she spoke. 'Your gran.' She nodded at me. 'She knew.'

'Knew what?' I was confused.

'She knew I'd felt something. She asked if I wanted to talk, and said that someone wanted to talk to me. So I ended up at her kitchen table that night and we talked for hours about energies, and spirits, and angels. For the first time in ages I felt good, I mean really good about myself. I knew I could ask her anything and she wouldn't judge me for not knowing. That was your gran's gift. She accepted people as they were, and in that fun way of hers, she coaxed you along. Being scared of what people thought or said about me sounds so silly now I'm saying it to you, but it was the way I felt. It was like everyone else was in charge of my life. I was a supporting actor in my own life, running round trying to keep everyone else happy.

'Then your gran asked if I wanted to meet my Guardian Angel. I did. I so wanted to find out what was there and feel that light in my head again, but I was really scared. I started to cry and she asked me why. She was so kind. I told her that I was really frightened. If angels were beings of light, what would they make of me? I felt such a failure in my life. I really couldn't imagine an angel having time for me, never mind loving me in the way she said they did.

'Your gran said that there was nothing we could do that would make our angels turn away from us. She said they loved us unconditionally, just for being us. Do you know how much I wanted to believe that? But it seemed unlikely. And I supposed I had a bit of an epiphany. I realised that all the people I loved, I did it with conditions. I had one of those moments in life where everything was clear. I could see all the relationships I had, including with Malcolm, and how I was continually setting conditions. I felt I had to do stuff for people to love me. I had never thought that I could be loved no matter what I did or didn't do.'

She paused to push her hair away from her face, and gave a gentle sigh. 'I don't know if I'm explaining it well enough to you, but it was as if a veil fell from my eyes. Like I could properly see my life and all my choices as just that. Choices. And because of that I suddenly knew that I could make other choices.

'Sitting at your gran's kitchen table, I said I was ready and she brought in some healing to me. It was like I felt a fluttering at my heart, and she said she sensed layers and layers of barbed wire which I'd constructed to keep myself safe from pain. But in doing that I'd created a barrier between me and life and love. She asked if I wanted to let it go, and I whispered that I did. I was crying again but it was like good tears, like I was releasing something sad in my heart and in my stomach.

'I had my eyes closed, and as she did that I started to see in my mind the image of a pair of large dark eyes. They were huge almond-shaped eyes, and I could see them looking at me with what I can say was pure love. Then the only way to describe it was I was aware of a sort of human-shaped creature appear around those eyes. I wasn't scared or anything. I didn't know if it was male or female; it was both and neither. I wasn't aware of colour either, but it was large and as if it floated and was opaque, not fully formed.'

Angel's eyes were shining now as she described her experience, and I could feel a real longing inside me to know more.

'It was a strange experience,' she went on, 'and I suppose part of me was thinking it was my imagination, but I focused on the expression in the eyes and it was beautiful. For the first time in my life I felt accepted, supported, admired, and I didn't have to do a thing. I saw it all in those eyes.

'Your gran whispered that this was my Guardian Angel and that she wanted to come closer to me so that I could feel her energy some more, that she was there to help me and always had been, my whole life. I must have nodded as I was aware of her, or it, coming closer in my mind but also in my senses. I felt arms coming around me – and this probably sounds crazy, or maybe you think it all does – it was as if there were feathers against my face. I could have sat there forever. I felt like I was surrounded by blessings of love.

'So that was it for me. I knew she was an angel. And I knew I didn't have to see her with my eyes, because she was an energy, so I felt her and saw her in a different way. She was an energy of love.'

'That sounds incredible!' I was almost lost for words. 'And my gran helped you with that?'

'Your gran did some amazing work.' Angel nodded. 'She worked with all types of energy, and she helped people feel better about their lives and their losses. She had an incredible way of supporting people practically as well as emotionally. This town has had her as an angel all these years. You've no idea.' She laughed again. 'She even found this place for me.'

'How did that happen?' I looked admiringly around the coffee shop. It was lovely, and now that I knew my gran had been involved I felt more peaceful.

'Well, after I met my Guardian Angel in your gran's kitchen, I went home and for the first time ever I looked at my life properly. I suppose you could say I re- evaluated my life. I started to talk to my angel throughout the day when I was in doubt, when I was worried, when I was stressed, or feeling lonely. And over the next few weeks my life started to change.

'I knew that I had to talk to Malcolm, but I also knew he wouldn't want to hear about my angel experience, so instead I asked if we could talk about us and our future. My angel told me not to blame him or me for our relationship, instead I was to trust that the right words would come to mind. And they did. We talked for hours about our lives, about what we wanted, and then about our relationship. I told him that I wanted things to change. I was able to say "living like this isn't honouring me", a word I had never used before but it felt so right.'

Angel's words hit me, and I suddenly realised that was how I had felt for so long. I wanted a life and a love which honoured me.

She went on with her story. 'Malcolm agreed that he hadn't been happy either, but that he wanted to separate. I was so shocked because I really hadn't thought it would have come to that, and I could feel the old fears flooding into my mind. But at that moment I had a sense of my Guardian Angel drawing near, and I felt Malcolm's angel as well. It was as if there were two conversations going on – Malcolm and I talking, and our two Guardian Angels communicating with each other as well. It was sad but okay.

'Malcolm moved out that night, and after a couple of months we sold the house. I knew I wanted to stay in the town, but I really didn't know what I wanted to do. My Guardian Angel told me to speak to my boss at the hospital. I was really worried about doing that, but I realised I had to trust her guidance, so I arranged to speak to my boss, and guess what? She offered me a redundancy package, as she wanted to reorganise staff. She told me that she had been worried about who to let go, as it would probably have been one of the younger team who hadn't been there as long as me. So I suppose my Guardian Angel helped that whole situation, and it all worked out beautifully for everyone.

'I was nearly fifty and didn't have a clue what I wanted to do, but again your gran came to help me. She arranged to meet me outside here when it was nothing but a partial ruin, and who came along the road at that very moment? Father Timothy, the priest for St Mary's, and a few minutes behind him, Davie Gallagher, a local builder. Your gran started a conversation with both of them about how wonderful it would be for St Mary's to have a coffee shop close by, and introduced me to the builder and Father Timothy, as the woman to set it up.

'It was the perfect idea and the ideal project for me. I heard myself agree. So within a few weeks we had all the planning sorted out, I'd bought the building with my proceeds from the house, and the flat above was made habitable. And here I am.' She looked proudly around the coffee. 'I added on the conservatory to create some brightness for people to sit in, the pews were already here, and I wanted to let people know about angels. So I started stocking and selling them, and of course your gran knew that I loved to bake cakes.

'Within a few months of meeting my Guardian Angel my life was completely transformed, and then I learned more from your gran about energy and healing. Now I like to share that knowledge with others, helping them to tune into their own wisdom by turning down the chatter in their heads. I run meditation classes and workshops on the Divine Feminine, all about honouring women and, in doing so, standing in our own power and enabling all around us to do so, too. I like the idea of a win-win society!' And with that she laughed again.

It was so inspiring to speak to someone who loved their work so much that I could feel it. I don't think I'd ever felt that. Work was sometimes interesting but never a passion. When Angel had stopped talking, the older lady who had been chatting to her at the counter came over, reached out her hand, and introduced herself in a very, cultured deep voice. 'Grizelle Hamilton-Brown. My dear, I am so sorry for your sadness, but that your grandmother is no longer on the earthly plane and instead can carry on her work in the higher realms, gives me great comfort..'

'What?' I almost choked on the last little crumb of cake I'd managed to eat while Angel was talking.

'What do you mean?' I stuttered. 'I'm sorry, I don't mean to be rude, but what did you say? Carrying on her work? What's that supposed to mean?'

I realised that my voice had risen and I could hear it bounce off the stone walls of the now empty coffee shop. The flickering candle-effect lights added to my 'out of this world' confusion. I felt so terribly emotional, not like my usual self, and I could hear my pulse beating loudly in my ears. I was sure if I stood up my legs would give way. My face must have paled, and at once Grizelle put a gentle hand on my shoulder.

'I don't want to distress you, my dear.' She looked briefly at Angel, and seemed to gain unspoken confirmation to carry on. 'There was something your grandmother undertook, some promises she made, and some work she did and still has to do...'

I could feel anger rising in me, outrage, panic, and the need to get away from this woman. It's funny how only a few words can completely change everything. I looked anxiously around the room, but there was no-one to intervene, or break up this crazy conversation.

'Please don't be angry.' Angel touched my hand gently. 'This might all sound mad to you, but we really have to talk.' I looked down at her hand where it touched mine, her nails neatly cut. 'We worked with your gran, we loved her, we promised to look out for you and help you... to tell you what was happening.'

There was something in her calm voice that reassured me. Deep down inside I knew they were not trying to scare me or anything like that. But I *was* scared. I had been ever since I'd heard the news of Granny's death, and the strange experiences of the last twenty-four hours had added to my distress.

There was a knot of fear somewhere inside me, and I didn't know why. I stood up more abruptly than I realised when I saw a look of surprise pass over their faces. *Maybe they were as scared as me.*

Angel stood up, too. 'We can come to your grandmother's house with you,' she offered. 'We'd love to help, and there will be things you'll have to do there.'

I knew that was a task I needed to face sometime, and something made me confide in them that I planned visiting the solicitor first, to get the keys and see what else I had to do.

Angel told me not to worry, and to take my time. 'Why don't you come and stay with me rather than the B&B? I've got a spare room. Please.' She seemed to sense my hesitance.

'Let me do it for your gran. Then we can help you with Kirsten's things when you feel ready.'

'But don't put it off too long,' added Grizelle. 'You're better to face these things sooner rather than later.'

I looked closely into both of their faces for a moment, and felt immediately calmer, less panicked, just from having them close. Neither of them was trying to upset me. I hadn't realised I had been holding my breath, but now I let it out with a long sigh. These two ladies were my granny's friends. They knew a lot more about her life than I did. They'd spent time with her and had information about her.

Something about Grizelle, and her voice especially, felt very familiar. With another deep breath I heard myself thanking them and agreeing to Angel's offer. I wasn't normally someone who acted hastily, but it was as if something inside told me to accept, and I couldn't disagree.

'Great.' Angel looked genuinely happy that I'd be staying with her. 'Pop back to the B&B and pack up your things and I'll come round and pick you up in about half an hour.'

Back at the B&B, Mrs Thomson refused to accept any money for my stay.

'Put your purse away, Kirsty, and don't be silly. I was at school with your gran and she was always a good friend. It's the least we can do. And let us know if you need any help at the cottage. We told her we'd look out for you.'

Words failed me, and tears filled my eyes as Mrs Thomson rubbed my arm, and gave me a quick hug.

8

Angel's old yellow VW Beetle sat at the gate, black fumes belching out from the exhaust. There were red flowers stencilled all across the bonnet and boot. 'This is such a cool car,' I told her, as I dropped my bag into the back seat and got in beside her.

'It's an original. It was refurbished about five years ago. Only needs a little work done and it'll be fine again.' Her obvious pride in the car stopped me pointing out the defective exhaust, which is what I would usually have done, and I decided to take shallow breaths instead.

Within minutes we were back at the coffee shop, and parked on the road at the front. She hustled me into a little side gate which I hadn't noticed, along a narrow path between the old stone walls of the coffee shop and the church, and into a beautiful little courtyard directly behind the building. Despite the winter weather, little bright green firs in pots sat along the edges of the yard. Other multi-coloured pots dotted around brought in the hues of spring and summer, like lavender, mint and other herbs and hardy plants.

An old wooden table and chairs sat to one side, and in the middle was some sort of brushwood structure standing about six feet tall. I thought at first it was a shed or a kids' play house, but as I got closer I realised it was pyramid-shaped. I glanced at Angel who smiled and lifted her eyebrows as if to say, 'What do you expect?'

Even as I asked if this was for children to play in, I knew it was hers.

'I use it to meditate in, and I put my plants in as it helps them grow. Because it's so close to the church, it's on an earth energy line so I believe it helps with healing the earth.'

I didn't have a clue where to start with my questions. I mean, a pyramid? In a back garden? I hadn't heard of energy lines either. And meditation? I didn't know anyone who did that, and had never tried. How do you stop your thoughts coming through, and did it really make any difference?

She gestured for me to follow her up the external stone staircase, potted plants lining the edges of the steps. In summer it would be beautiful and I could imagine all the colourful flowers trailing down the stairs. A sharp, icy cold wind caught me as I got to the top, sending a chill through my entire body and a horrible feeling of fear straight to my stomach. It surprised me, as the courtyard seemed so sheltered set between the coffee shop and the church walls.

By the time I stepped into the flat, Angel was rushing round lighting lamps, candles, and logs in the stove. The early evening darkness was hidden behind thick red curtains, but not before I caught a glimpse of the church, floodlit and ethereally framed for a moment in the window like a magnificent oil painting in a too tight frame.

I followed her through to her spare bedroom. All the rooms led off the big but cosy square lounge. In front of the stove were two large red sofas laden with bright cushions and tartan throws to keep out the chill. Big bookcases, crammed to overflowing with all shapes and sizes of books and magazines, stood on both sides of the stove which sat on a black granite hearth at the corner of the room. It was already throwing out heat and light into the chilly air.

The spare bedroom was lovely, with the same dark wooden floor, exposed stone walls like the downstairs cafe, and a small leaded glass window overlooking the courtyard and the church. It was stunning, and I felt strangely comforted that it sat there and was almost watching over me at such a strange time in my life.

Angel switched on the bedside lamp, and the huge brass bed glinted in the light. I took out my toiletries and night things and pushed my bag under the bed. She had returned to the kitchen and I heard her calling me. By the time I got there she had the Aga on, and the kitchen had lost its chill. She looked surprised to see me.

'I thought you might be taking a bath or something,' she said.

'I think I'm too tired even for that. But you called me.'

Angel looked at me strangely. 'No, I didn't.'

'Someone did…'

That awful feeling of dread hit me again and, despite the warmth of the room and the cosy surroundings, it was like I was being watched – or worse, hunted. I shrugged off that feeling. It was my imagination, nothing more. This was my first bereavement as an adult and it had unsettled me, that was all. There was nothing else to worry about.

I ignored a little doubting niggle deep in my body, and instead concentrated on the food which Angel had heated up. It was easier than admitting that I felt unsettled. We had a delicious veggie hotpot, with more bread and butter, and I found an appetite from somewhere, even managing a big chunk of chocolate cake. Eventually we settled onto the sofas in front of the roaring stove in the lounge with cups of tea. I had eaten too much and felt sleepy.

I had a feeling she wanted to talk about my gran, but I didn't want to get upset again, so I asked her about the pyramid outside. She told me it enhanced meditation, and that she had covered it with brushwood so that she could sit in it even on the coldest, wettest day. Seeing my puzzled face, she offered me a book to look at later.

'I meditate a couple of times a day,' she explained. 'Sitting in the energies of the pyramid with my crystals makes me feel good.'

'How do you do it? I don't see how you can stop your thoughts. I wouldn't be able to. And does it really work? I mean… how does it work?'

Angel sipped her tea then smiled. 'I've been doing it for a couple of years now, and like opening myself up to Angels and energies, life has just got better and better. I love my life and feel really fulfilled in what I do. I never ever dreamed of a different life. I realise now that I didn't dare. It was like there was a part of me that wanted to break out and experience something different, but the rest of me bit it back and wouldn't let it out. Like the little girl in me knew there could be a happy ending, but the adult part of me wouldn't let her speak. Does that make any sense to you?'

Strangely it did. I had a fleeting sense of a whisper of a child inside me as she spoke. I nodded my agreement, as I was finding this all fascinating. I'd had no idea that there was another way.

'So I meditate every day. I wake in the morning and connect with my Higher Self, and thank the Universe for all the blessings on my day, and then I check in with her during the day, and at night I send out my appreciation to all for my life and all the wonderful experiences I have.'

'Your Higher Self? What do you mean, Angel? And how can you give thanks in advance for your day when you don't know how good or bad it's going to be?' I asked her, my brow wrinkling in confusion.

'That's the whole point, Kirsty. Life is always a blessing. It's us that can't always see it. We fill our heads with all sorts of negative thoughts, and keep ourselves busy as a distraction. We're the ones who bring judgement into our lives. We decide whether something is good or bad.

'I learned that life is neutral. We make our choices based on what we expect to happen. Think about the things we tell ourselves. The negative stories we tell ourselves and, if you think about it, how we restrict ourselves by deciding in advance that there can only be an outcome that we create. My life is so much easier now that I leave all that to the Universe. I realised that I wasn't letting anything good happen to me. I had already decided that life was going to be bad, and get worse. In doing that, I was trying to control everything. Negative thoughts bring in more negativity. Positive thoughts from a grateful heart can change lives. Look what happened to me.'

I struggled a bit to get my head around what she meant. But there felt like a little nugget of wisdom in what she said, and it was good to hear about her new life.

She continued, 'Scientists are now discovering in experiments on the human brain that meditation slows down the frequency of brainwaves and can take the person into a dreamlike state of mind. This enhances creativity and relaxation and reduces stress levels. I believe that if people found out how good meditation can make you feel, they would have no need to take drugs or get drunk all the time. I'd love to teach it in prisons, can you imagine the difference that would make in society? Everyone peaceful, calm and creative, with no need to steal or cause harm. For me, I feel I go somewhere special and into a feeling of bliss.'

Bliss. At will, or rather, when you wanted it. That sounded amazing to me. I asked her about the pyramid again.

'You're welcome to use it. There's a crystal grid layout inside and some little lamps. Pop in tomorrow, lie down and daydream'

'Is daydreaming the same as meditation?' I asked.

'Similar brain patterns,' she said, 'but sometimes it's nice to empty your mind and… well, you'll find out, I'm sure. First things first.'

'What do you do with crystals?' I asked. 'I remember Gran having some large crystals which I'm sure she said were Scottish, but she liked to keep them in the garden rather than the house. I knew she felt that they shouldn't be dug up.'

'Hmm,' said Angel, 'your gran and I had slightly different views on using crystals. She felt that they should all be returned to the earth, and I agreed to a certain level. But if crystals can help us and they are already available, then why not use them? I work with many different crystals, as they all have specific properties, and I love their energy.'

There was that word again. Energy. I wasn't exactly sure what she meant, but didn't want to interrupt. She offered me a huge piece of purple amethyst which was sitting at the side of her sofa, so I hadn't seen it when we sat down. It was the size of a football, and as she turned it around I realised it was cut into the shape of a skull. I thought it was horrible, really frightening. She could tell what I was thinking from my face.

'There's no need to be scared. The crystal skulls are here to provide real help to us right now. You'll see more and more of them over the next few years as people lose fear and accept their power more.'

This was too freaky for words, but I didn't want to admit that I was scared of it. Instead, I opened my arms and nestled it against my chest. Instantly I felt like a tremor, a slight vibration against my skin. It was like being plugged into a power source of some kind, like a gigantic purple battery.

'Close your eyes and lie back against the cushions,' suggested Angel.

As much as I didn't want to do that, I felt to say no would be to admit that I was scared. So I did as she suggested and closed my eyes. It was weird. Part of me knew I was sitting on the sofa in front of the flames, but it was my imagination that fired up. It was as if the crystal was communicating with me. I sensed something in it or around it. Nothing frightening;

instead it was like a softness. Like it wanted to comfort my heart.

I remembered years before, holidaying in Mexico and swimming with the dolphins. I had forgotten how connected I felt to them. Like they were wanting us to laugh and smile. And we all did. Everyone in the group was laughing and the dolphins laughed back. This was the same experience. The crystal skull was communicating with me. It wanted to show me something, and into my mind came Gran, smiling at me. She blew me a kiss like she used to do, and laughed.

I quickly opened my eyes to find Angel watching me intently. She said nothing and passed me another crystal. 'Smoky quartz,' she said. 'It clears negativity.'

It was shaped like a dragon's head, and the size of a melon. It was heavy, and instead of holding it against my chest I moved it over my stomach. I closed my eyes without prompting and again felt a tingle. High in my tummy area I felt heat from the crystal. It was trying to tell me something. 'It's time,' I heard, or sensed, or just knew. 'Time for action. We are here. Don't be afraid. We are with you.'

Again I opened my eyes. As odd as that had been, I actually didn't feel afraid. Angel sat across from me holding a large pink stone against her heart. She must have sensed I was watching her and introduced me to her piece of pink quartz. 'It's for universal healing,' she said, 'and the colour of the heart.'

I told her about the two experiences, and she just smiled and nodded. She explained that she believed the crystals communicated with us when we chose to listen.

All of this was so new to me, and I wasn't sure how I felt about it all. My mind went back to something she had mentioned earlier.

'What did you mean about "healing the earth"?' I asked.

'A lot of people around the world are now aware of the distress humans have caused to the planet,' she replied, 'and they use whatever means they can to put positive energies into the earth, particularly in areas of conflict, stress, or environmental damage. We use meditation, crystals, sacred sound, and send love to Mother Earth.'

'Send love?' I asked.

'We can love our planet, and as we become aware of the spiritual beings we are, connect with the elementals, nature, and other energy bodies.'

'How do you know other people are doing it?'

'We just do, and there is now so much information on the internet so we can all come together. The more people meditating at the same time, the more powerful the outcome, and we can communicate and spread the love.'

I felt a little embarrassed at all this talk of love. It wasn't my usual topic of conversation, especially given my recent break-up. I suppose I had only ever really thought about romantic love and love for my granny, which felt different. I'd never really considered love in any other form, especially about the earth, although I realised that's exactly what Gran had done and had tried to talk to me about.

'Is this like the peace protesters, and environmentalists, and all the new age stuff you read about and see in the news?' I sipped my tea, trying to make sense of what she was telling me.

'That's one part of it,' Angel explained, 'but also people want to do something good, to compensate for all the years of stripping the earth of its natural resources, and as well as that, to connect with each other, to find a higher purpose for life.'

'But you said you did it in places of stress or conflict, do you mean like war zones?'

'Yes, we all send love to places in the world that need it,' she said.

'Okay.' I let her words sink in. 'That's really interesting, and I can understand that people would want to try and send good thoughts to places like that, but... I suppose my question is, why here?'

My words hung in the air between us like an invisible barrier. She looked really shocked. I had no idea why my words had such an effect, but it was obvious that they did.

Angel took a deep breath and started to mess about with the fire, adding more logs. She didn't look at me for a couple of minutes, almost as though she was trying to compose herself.

She let out a long slow breath and turned back to face me. 'I would prefer Grizelle to be with us to talk about all this, she can tell you a lot more about the history of the town. And I'm sure she could answer all your questions. Did you hear that only a couple of miles from us is an open cast mine? The company won the rights to extend their excavations to within a few miles of the town, which you know is a World Heritage site. Even the March Stones will be affected.'

'Surely not?' It was my turn to be shocked. 'Everyone in the town knows that the stones aren't supposed to be touched. Is there not a legend that something will happen to Scotland if anything happens to the stones? Or is that a story they thought up for the tourists?'

The town was famed for its week-long festivities every June, including a parade, marching bands, horse riders, bandsmen, dances, and the famous 'Marches' – a walk by the whole town around its perimeter to inspect the March Stones. This had been done every year for centuries, and the festival and ceremony brought thousands of visitors to the town.

'What is the town doing about it? Will the council let the extension go through?' I asked her.

'It's out of their hands now, all decisions like that are taken at the council's regional headquarters, and they are probably thinking about safeguarding employment rather than a place of natural beauty and an old legend. Some people say that the councillors and planning department are receiving bribes –things like golfing trips and holidays — from the owners of the mine,' said Angel.

'Surely that can't be legal?'

'Well, I suppose if they dress it up like fact-finding trips then no-one is the wiser! But we got lucky – or should I say, your gran knew one of the ladies who worked in planning at the local council offices. She told her everything, including that the permission would go through, the stones would be shifted, and even the names of the officials involved.'

I felt sick. 'Would that have put my gran in danger?' Even as I whispered the words, I felt a cold chill and the lights flickered as if in response.

I could see Angel was really worried, too. The temperature in the room had dropped, and she jumped up to put on another log. I also noticed that her body language had changed again, as if she was avoiding looking me in the eye.

'How much was my gran involved in this? I'm sure she had something to say about it all, after all we have one of the March Stones on our property. We had the first stone, Gran said. The other twelve stones are around the town, and the last one, the thirteenth was about a mile from us, at the quarry. It used to be such fun seeing the entire town appearing all together as they inspected each stone to make sure they were in place. Our house and garden used to be crazy during the Marches, as we had to give refreshments Granny used to be baking for a week beforehand.'

At the mention again of my gran, Angel jumped up and made some comments about being tired and past her bed-time, and suggesting we could talk more in the morning.

I had no choice but to agree, so I headed to her spare room. 'Thanks again for having me, Angel,' I said sincerely. 'I hope I get a better sleep than last night.'

'Goodnight, Kirsty,' she said with a gentle smile. 'Don't worry. I have asked Archangel Michael to come in and watch you while you sleep, and the house is surrounded by angels keeping a watchful eye on us.'

That made me smile, but also gave me some comfort.

9

Something worked for me. I slept soundly all night, the best in weeks; no strange dreams, sensations, sounds or feelings, and I woke up early to the sound of the church bells and the smell of baked scones. I pulled on my dressing gown and headed into the kitchen. Angel had already left to open up her business, and underneath a warm blueberry muffin there was a note to say she would be downstairs.

I took my time showering, and trying to sort out my hair so I looked less wild woman, and more groomed than over the last few days. I popped the kettle on and had some tea and toast, sitting in front of breakfast television like it was a holiday.

Although this was the most rested I'd felt in ages, my shoulders ached with tension, and I knew I couldn't put off visiting Granny's house. I found my mobile phone in the bottom of my handbag, still on silent from the service yesterday. I had some missed calls and texts from friends in London, so I replied to them to let everyone know I was okay. At least at that moment I felt okay, but the thought of going to the house was worrying me, and my jaw ached with tension.

My phone pipped again with a text from Derek. I didn't really want to read it, worried that it would be something horrible, but instead it said he was sorry. He said he had made a big mistake, and he loved me. I felt tears come into my eyes as I held it to my heart. I realised I wanted him to want me, but I didn't know what I felt about him any more.

The last few weeks apart had shown me that it had always been all about him. Not his fault or anything, but I hadn't been true to myself. I'd always compromised, which meant I'd always yielded in an attempt to avoid conflict. Even when I'd left I hadn't been honest about how I felt. I'd left quietly and easily like a mouse. No wonder I felt such shame and hadn't wanted to tell my gran.

I decided not to reply immediately. I really didn't know what to say to him. Instead, I called Granny's solicitor, Mr Douglas. He answered on the first ring, and we arranged for me to go down to his office right away. He had the will ready, and the keys to Granny's house.

A few minutes later I was out of the door, wrapped up warmly in coat, scarf and gloves, and ran down to let Angel know my plans. The sharp wind had died down from the night before, and the courtyard was still and silent as I hurried past the pyramid, down the passageway, and through the gate into the coffee shop. Angel was busy with customers, but waved me over to the counter and said she would be ready to go whenever I arrived back with the keys. I was so grateful that she remembered, as I had been dreading asking her.

The solicitor's office was at the bottom of the High Street. I headed downhill into a cold, damp, foggy morning, and noticed another little white moth fluttering away in front of me. So strange to see another one in the daylight; I'd never noticed that before.

I was soon sitting across from Mr Douglas at his big mahogany desk. A very large painting of the local waterfall was on the wall behind his head, and I felt my eyes flicker back and forward between it and the solicitor. He had known me all my life, but I'd never sat in his office on my own before. I had no idea what age he was, as he'd always looked the same – tall, slim, and dressed formally in a pin-striped suit, with waist-coat, shirt and tie.

Last time I had been here was with Gran; I might have been ten or eleven. I've no idea what it was about, lots of adult talk I suppose, then we had gone for ice creams at the Italian café across the road. It had closed down years ago. They made their ice cream on the premises. It was always a great treat to sit there with a bowl of vanilla ice cream and raspberry sauce, eaten with the tiniest little spoon so that it lasted for ages.

I suddenly realised that Mr Douglas had been speaking, and was now looking at me expectantly as his little speech came to an end. I apologised and told him how difficult I was finding it all, being back in the town, and everyone's kindness.

I suppose I knew or expected that everything had been left to me. With some bequests to local charities, the house and gardens were mine, and he thought there would be a sizeable inheritance once the estate was finally settled. He was waiting for some information on some stocks Granny had held, and then he handed me a big set of keys. To be more precise, he handed me a set of big keys. Big, old-fashioned keys for big, old-fashioned locks. I felt like a jailer as I pushed them to the bottom of my handbag.

I suppose I had thought Gran would have left me a personal letter. The will was all official language and there didn't seem to be anything of my grandmother in it. She might have taken care of all her affairs and organised her funeral, but I was still sure she hadn't expected to pass away that particular night. If she had, surely she would have left me a note or called me or something.

I tried to remember our last conversation and how normal it had been. I had been distracted, I remember. She had called me at work, which was really unusual, and I said I'd call her back. I felt sick as I realised that was the night before she died.

She had wanted to talk to me. I felt tears again, and a feeling of shame. She had wanted to talk to me, but I hadn't taken the time to talk to her.

And here I was inheriting everything. I had to get out of the office and be on my own, so I shook the solicitor's hand and thanked him again. As he walked me to the door, I asked him one final question.

'Mr Douglas, I didn't get a chance to thank you for making all the arrangements. And I forgot to ask... this probably sounds terrible, but who found Gran... after... she... you know?'

I whispered and felt my voice give up. I couldn't say the word 'died'; it was too soon, too hard.

Mr Douglas cleared his throat and seemed to look everywhere but at me, probably giving me a few minutes to compose myself. He probably didn't want me bawling my eyes out here in his outer office and doorway to the street.

'Kirsty, I have to apologise. I thought you were told all this. Doctor McLeod found your gran, he'll have all the details. You might want to talk to him. And your gran made all her own arrangements. She came in and saw me a week or so before she died, to tie up all the loose ends, as she said! I was surprised that she passed away so suddenly after that, but you know what she was like... with her visions and everything.'

I was really surprised to hear Mr Douglas refer to Granny's intuition. I supposed being a lawyer he would have probably have ignored that kind of thing. And was it really surprising that Gran wouldn't have known that it was her time? It was so like her to organise things. But I hadn't known she was ill. Why else would the doctor have come to her?

I felt terrible. Granny had been ill and I hadn't known. Shame and grief hit me in equal parts, and I left Mr Douglas quite abruptly, hoping he would understand. I headed back up the High Street towards *Angel's Cakes*, sadness again settling on my aching shoulders. Perhaps Granny had called me that day to tell me she was ill and dying. What had I been doing that was so important that I hadn't called her back? Work. And avoiding her because I was so embarrassed about Derek. I hadn't wanted to tell her. No wonder I felt so bad. Guilt and shame, that's what I felt, and sick to the stomach.

As the tears filled my eyes, I heard someone call my name and saw Grizelle waving at me from the doorway of a shop on the other side of the road.

Of course, that's who she is! Suddenly I remembered where I knew her face from. She had the antiques shop, *Serendipity*, near *The Three Keys*. Not that it was the kind of shop I ever used to visit. It was crammed with stuff. The kind of place I got nervous in just in case I knocked over something valuable.

Behind her, the shop looked dark and packed full with chairs, tea sets, rugs, lamps, a couple of grandfather clocks, a piano, and I could even see a stag's head hanging on the wall.

She seemed to know I was upset and tried to offer me tea, but I turned her down and explained what I planned to do with Angel. I couldn't shake the feeling that if I went inside her shop, all the collectables would become breakables. *Funny how we hold onto childhood fears*, I thought.

I really didn't want to talk about how I felt with anyone. I knew I had to keep busy. For me, that was the only way to get through life.

Reluctantly, she let me go and I heard her calling after: 'Take care. Sending you lots of love.' There was something about that voice that still made me feel anxious, but I didn't know why. I had a sense that I'd heard it somewhere before, a long time ago. *Perhaps at Granny's house? Was that it? Why couldn't I remember?*

As I crossed the road towards the coffee shop, I saw James Jack the undertaker and his father, John, coming towards me. They were practically identical in their black-tailed suits and waistcoats, and tall hats. The street was too narrow to avoid them and I knew that Granny would have expected me to thank them for their service. I would also have to see the minister and the doctor, a little voice whispered in my ear.

'Hi there, thanks for everything… You were so helpful,' I said.

The older man shook my hand, pressed my arm and said how sorry he was to lose Granny. 'She was like a mother to me. Always so kind and caring to people. We'll all miss her.'

James interrupted, 'And how amazing that she came in only a couple of days before and booked everything! I was really shocked when we got the call from Dr McLeod, wasn't I, Dad? And you just said, "that would be unbelievable, except that we're talking about Kirsten Wallace", didn't you, Dad?'

I could hardly believe it myself.

'Sorry, what? My gran came in and booked the funeral recently? I thought it was something she'd done ages ago with no definite date in mind…' I sounded so feeble, so pathetic. *Did it really matter?* My gran did know it was her time, that was obvious. And she had been ill, yet I hadn't known.

The Jacks said how sorry they were again and, with another squeeze of consolation and sympathy on my arm, they were gone in the grey drizzle, cutting across the busy road to their premises.

I felt pathetic by the time I reached Angel's, and she insisted I have some food whilst she handed over to one of her staff members, a lovely looking young girl with fashionable, thick, black eyebrows, eyeliner, and pink spiked hair.

I sat and flicked through a magazine and had lentil soup and a toasted cheese sandwich, and a couple of cups of tea. The food, time out, and angels around me, all worked their magic and I felt better more able to face going to the cottage. Or at least I had the physical strength to go, but my heart and head were somewhere else.

If only I could stop these thoughts of regret, of sadness, guilt and shame. If only I had known what was going to happen. If only I'd known she was leaving me, how different things would have been. I could have told her how much she meant to me. I wondered if she knew that. If only I'd known, I would have come home sooner. What I would give to see her face, hear her voice one more time. To hold her in my arms and tell her I loved her. I felt so ashamed, and my eyes filled with tears of sadness.

10

Granny's house sat on the other side of the graveyard from the church and the town. Her garden sloped very steeply down to the River Clyde below. The river started high in the hills behind her house, dropping hundreds of feet in three large waterfalls to the old mills across the river. We had occasional glimpses during winter when the dense woods on the opposite bank dropped their leaves. Sometimes, in a particularly cold spell, the waterfalls would ice up completely and there would be silence rather than the distant sound of rushing water.

My heart was beating fast when we got out of Angel's car, and I pushed open the squeaky iron gate in the low wall, hand-built from old stones by one of my ancestors. Although she had died only a week ago, the gardens and house had already taken on an abandoned look.

Granny was born and died in this house, like her mother before her, and her mother before her, and so on. This house was part of my family, and I struggled with feelings of guilt and shame as I walked towards the door. It was a long time since I'd visited. Life in London kept me busy, and as much as I spoke to Gran often, it had been ages since I'd seen her. Not speaking to her on the night she died was a secret shame I couldn't share. *Maybe that's why I was so unsettled*, I thought. Old-fashioned guilt.

As I walked through the garden, I realised that it was now mine, and I didn't have a clue what I would do with the place. So many memories; some painful, some fun, and all with Gran. I caught a flutter of white wings at the corner of my vision and as I turned towards the moth to try to see it better, Angel again seemed to read my thoughts.

'What do you think you want to do with the place?' she asked.

I shook my head and shrugged my shoulders, misery settling over me.

The house had originally been on one level – two rooms and a kitchen and bathroom downstairs, with an attic. The attic, over time, had then modelled into two bedrooms – one for me and one for my mum. I didn't remember my dad ever living there; actually, I don't remember him at all. I hardly remembered Mum living here.

That's strange, I thought, *my memories are really only of me and Gran*. She slept downstairs in a small bedroom at the back of the house. It sat in large grounds, with the graveyard in front, the woods and river at the back, and fields on either side. We had no neighbours, and I used to love that. But this time it felt isolated, and lonely. *Or was feeling that coming from me?*

I used to love this place. The garden had been an adventure land to me and my school friends, full of trees and shrubs, places to hide, and trees to swing from. We'd had our own little stone bridge across a stream in the garden. Gran called it the 'Roman Bridge', as supposedly the Romans had set up a large camp nearby.

And we had one of the ancient March Stones as well, so every year we entertained the town as they marched round the perimeter stones. Granny called us the Guardians of the Stone, which always seemed overly dramatic to me. Our family name of Cairngeal was supposed to be Scottish Gaelic – the old language – for guardian. Funny how I hadn't thought of that in years.

We walked slowly up the gravel path, our feet crunching in time, aware of the echo off the white-washed walls. Close up, the cottage was in good condition, so I had no idea why I thought it looked abandoned. The white paintwork round the windows was fresh and crisp, the door red and glossy, the brasses glinting and polished. To the side of the house, the vegetable and herb garden, and plant pots with winter pansies all looked smart and well cared for, as if Granny had just stepped out for a moment. I saw two white butterflies meander in and out of the pots.

'Do you see those?' I asked Angel. 'Are they moths or butterflies?'

'I think it's a sign,' she said.

'A sign? Of what?'

'Spirit... soul... angels... It's like when I see white feathers, I know the angels are around me.'

'I don't believe in signs,' I said dismissively. 'They must be special types of moths. You can't get butterflies in the winter. It's not possible.'

We turned back towards the door and I realised that I wanted, no, I expected Gran to open the door, smiling and reaching out to hug me tight. The realisation that it would never ever happen again hurt deeply, as if for the first time. I swallowed, took in a long breath, and pulled the keys out of my bag. I'd never had to unlock that door before. It had always been open, as if she knew I was coming.

As that thought came into my head, Angel and I realised that the door was indeed lying slightly open, obviously unlocked. We looked at each other in surprise. For a moment I thought Gran was waiting for us, had heard us come up the path, and had left the door ajar, like she always did. That she wasn't dead. That it had all been a mistake.

Angel pushed the door open fully and walked in first, as if she wanted to block my view for some reason. I followed her in, and gasped out loud. The door opened straight into the kitchen – Gran's usually immaculate, well ordered, clean and tidy kitchen.

But this kitchen was in complete disarray, as if a mini whirlwind had unleashed itself in this small space. I could see through into the lounge, and everything there was tidy and neat.

In the kitchen the copper pots were on the floor, and broken plates, cups and glasses littered the flagstones. The walls were empty, pictures and photos now smashed on the ground. Cupboard doors hung off hinges, drawers pulled out and contents spilled.

'Oh no!' I finally found my voice. 'Who would do this? Who would do this?'

Tears sprang to my eyes. How could a burglar have done this to my gran, her memory? As I bent down to pick up a photo of me, Mum and Gran, which usually sat on the windowsill, Angel seemed to spring to action. She grabbed a large tub of salt lying by the sink and frantically emptied some of it onto the floor in some sort of manic, crazy pattern.

Before I could ask her what she was doing, she ran past me through the lounge, pouring salt along the window ledges and door frames, then she ran back to the kitchen and did the same on the way back outside. I knew she was mumbling something but I couldn't catch what she said. I chased her outside and saw that she had her arms around the big rowan tree in the middle of the garden, talking to it, or singing at it. I saw her mouth move but couldn't hear properly.

'Angel, what are you doing?' But she either didn't hear me or ignored me.

Her hair was wild, her face set in a mask. As I got closer, she was making sounds like chants but not a song I'd ever heard. This was almost animalistic, primeval.

She stopped suddenly, as if she was listening to someone or something, and then ran behind the tree into the shrubbery. I didn't have a clue what was happening, but with the burglary, I was terrified and didn't want to let her out of my sight, even though it looked like she had lost her mind. By the time I reached her behind the tree, she was down on the ground, pushing and pulling at a huge stone. It was the March Stone – at least three feet square, and goodness knows how deep underground it went. Made of a shiny grey stone like granite, or something, it had strange markings carved or scratched all over it, swirls and spirals. Gran always said it had been put there by the Doonies, Scottish fairies, which always made me laugh.

Now, though, this was too bizarre. The stone had been moved. This huge rock that was part of this town's heritage and solidly set deep into the ground, had shifted.

Angel was trying to push it back into place. We could see a gaping hole, a dark chasm in the earth. She was straining to move it back, and a feeling of panic over took me. Whether it was adrenalin or something else, I sent up a silent prayer to whoever could help, and joined Angel on the frozen ground, seizing the stone and pushing with all my might.

There was no way that two average-sized women should have been able to move that stone, but move it we did; like magic it slid back into position. It was almost like invisible helpers had appeared and joined with us to settle it into the position it had held for thousands of years.

Angel's face was white with shock and panic, probably mirroring mine. I heard her giving thanks to someone or something for helping us, and I searched her face for answers. Words failed me, and as my heartbeat returned to normal, I had a feeling that some sort of disaster had been averted. I knew nothing. I had no idea what had happened, but I was scared. I could feel fear in the hairs at the back of my neck. Across the back of my shoulders, tendons and muscles had started to ache. As my body began to cool down rapidly in the chilled air, I could see my breath misting around me. Linking arms for comfort and strength, we walked back towards the house and though the door into the kitchen.

Unbelievably, the kitchen was now back to its usual tidy self; pristine, clean, organised, the way Granny always kept it. Not a thing out of place. The family photos sat on the window ledge, the pots, pans, crockery and glasses on their shelves. The cupboard doors and drawers were all back in place. The only thing on the floor was the pattern in salt which Angel had poured. It looked like some sort of star, a five-sided star, surrounded by a circle.

Protection was the word that suddenly flashed into my mind. Looking around the room, mouth open, I wanted to cry. This was too much to take in. I felt like my grip on reality had faded away. Like it was a living nightmare, but I knew I wasn't going to wake up in my bed.

'Angel, please just tell me, what's happening?'

11

Within minutes we were sitting round Granny's table, the kettle was on, and Grizelle was on her way after a muffled call from Angel. I sat there, not really comprehending what had happened. I knew I'd experienced it, but some part of me was still processing it, and my emotions hadn't yet caught up. It was as if I had disassociated from my body in some way. The weird thing was that I felt I had done it before.

Time seemed to speed up, and Grizelle arrived really quickly, as if on a broomstick. Then I thought that might be too close to the truth. *I mean, what was really going on?*

Grizelle was her usual calm, polite self. She gave me a hug and joined us at the table. Angel poured some tea, and Grizelle started to speak. She told me that she, Gran, and some others had 'worked' together for a long time to keep things safe. She asked me not to interrupt and that she'd try to tell me things in some sort of order. She wanted to start with my mother, for some strange reason.

I had a moment of clarity, like a memory from far away bounced into my head. I blurted out, 'That's where I've heard your voice before. You were here in this house the night my mum died. I heard you. I heard Mum shouting for me. She was asking me to help her.'

My voice broke, and with some shock I realised that I wanted to cry for the little girl I had been, and the guilt I felt because I hadn't been able to help my mum when she needed me.

'I heard voices, so I sneaked out of bed and spied from the top of the stairs. Mum was shouting and crying, and you were asking her to calm down and be sensible. Gran was talking, and Mum started to scream for me then she ran out of the cottage. Someone ran after her. I could hear them shouting.'

Tears were running down my face as that far away nightmare came into my mind in total clarity for the first time in years. 'Mum was crying. She was really upset.'

In my mind I could hear her screams of fear, real terror. She looked like the woman at the grave – long hair, green eyes, looking like Granny. It had been raining hard that night. The noise of the rain on the roof in the attic must have woken me up, or perhaps it was the voices I'd heard. They'd got louder as I came out of my bedroom. I'd sat at the top of the stairs in the dark, on the wooden steps, hugging the banister and trying to see down towards the kitchen. I could hear adults talking. I couldn't see anything, but I knew they were angry. I heard my gran, my mum and a deeper voice. No, they hadn't all been angry. It was Mum, she was shouting at the others. She was saying she couldn't do it, 'Please don't make me. I can't. We're going away. I won't do it.' I remember being so frightened.

I snapped back to reality. 'Grizelle, please tell me what happened.'

Grizelle looked at me with tears in her eyes, clearly moved by my distress. 'Kirsty, darling Kirsty. I wasn't here that night. It wasn't me you heard, but I can tell you what I know of it.'

'If it wasn't you, then who was it? Who did I hear? I couldn't see anybody, I was really scared.'

Grizelle took a deep breath. 'You heard your father, Kirsty. Your dad was trying to reason with your mum. Your gran had told her that she had a destiny to look out for the stones, but your mum was scared and didn't want to do it. She ran off, but that wasn't the night she died.'

'What? That can't be true. My dad died when I was a baby. He never lived here with us. That *was* the night Mum died, I'm sure of it. She was calling for me then she ran out. It was raining, I remember that. I thought it was my fault because I was too scared to help her.' The words hurt me as they pushed their way out. I struggled to hold myself together, feeling a sadness overwhelm me. A sadness I hadn't even known was there.

'Kirsty, listen to me. Yes, your mum did run out of the house that night. She ran a couple of miles to Hyndford Bridge, the oldest bridge in the town. Your dad found her hours later, huddled under the bridge. She was soaked to the skin. He wasn't sure if she had tried to drown herself, or whether it was the rain. He found her, they took her to hospital, and then she was committed to an asylum when she started to talk about spirits and such like.'

I looked from one to the other, then swallowed. 'I thought I saw someone who looked like her at Granny's grave yesterday,' I whispered. 'Is she alive then?'

'I'm sorry, Kirsty, she died about ten years ago. She never regained her sanity, I suppose you could say. She had always been a bit sensitive and she didn't want any part of this.' Grizelle gestured round the room.

I knew she wasn't talking about bricks and mortar. She was talking about something much deeper than that.

'I thought my dad had died when I was a baby. No-one ever mentioned him.'

'He left to go back to Ireland a few years after your mother went into hospital. I don't think anyone has seen him since, although I know he was in touch with your gran.'

'Why didn't Gran tell me any of this? How could she have let me believe Mum and Dad were dead? Is he still alive? I didn't know he lived in Ireland. So many years have passed. I don't know anything about him.' My mind was racing, struggling to take it all in.

'He came from Ireland, from a place called Drogheda. His is an old Celtic family, as is yours. They are also Guardians… Cairngeal… His family live close to Newgrange, an ancient Stone Age cairn. It's believed to be a temple to the sun. It has now been renovated but when it was a ruin, your father played with the stones as a child.' Grizelle paused briefly. 'I don't know where he is now. '

The significance of this was lost on me until much later.

Grizelle and Angel exchanged another glance, and Angel leaned over the table and put her hand on my arm, patting me. I felt the heat from her hand through my clothes.

'Kirsty, you wouldn't hear a word about your mum or your dad when you were young, so your gran didn't want to upset you by mentioning them. She took you to lots of doctors to try to help, but you were the one who said they were dead. Maybe it was easier for you to think that way. Your gran did try to talk to you…'

I looked at them in disbelief. 'Why would I do that? It doesn't make sense. Gran used to talk to me about Mum and show me photos. Why would I say she was dead when she wasn't? It doesn't make sense…'

'I think your gran was trying to keep your mum's memory alive,' Angel said, 'and hoped that there would be some sort of reconciliation. Unfortunately your mum's mental state got worse and she died suddenly.'

'Died suddenly? What do you mean?'

'I'm sorry to be the one to break this news to you. As your gran's oldest friend, I can tell you that she was always looking for the right time to tell you, but she said you would always change the subject, and it went on so long that she didn't know how to tell you that your memories of that time were

all mixed up. Your mum lived in a hospital for people with…
mental health issues. She fell from the window. They didn't
know if it was an accident or not, but she had been unwell for
a long time. She was always confused, scared about life. She
had always been anxious, from when she was little.'

*Could that really be the case? Could I have misremembered the
most important time of my childhood?* I sat with my head in my
hands, weary, confused and shocked. My brain just couldn't
take it all in. I had the separation feeling in my head again.
Like everything was at a distance from me.

'You said something about guarding the stones? If that's
so… how could that one have moved today, Angel? How
could a stone that size move? Is this something to do with
Gran dying? How could anyone have moved it?'

'Kirsty, we do have to talk about what's been happening
recently, and about your gran, and the stones.' Grizelle spoke
first, in her deepest most solemn tone. Her eyes were full of
support for me, and I knew she didn't want to hurt me. 'Your
family has had a very important role in the survival of this
town, and this town has had an important role in wider issues,
shall we say. I don't believe the stone was moved from above.'

For the first time in my life I knew what people meant
when they said words hung in the air. The room felt cold. I
was aware of a shiver running through me. It started somewhere in my toes and finished at the top of my spine. Angel
looked behind her and out of the window.

Darkness had arrived, but the moon sent silver light and
shadows through heavy clouds to play across the room.
Whilst Grizelle was talking, she lit the large candle sitting in
the middle of the table so that we weren't in total darkness.
The flame flickered with invisible draughts, wax slowly sliding down the candlestick, and pooling on the old wooden
table top. We'd spent so much time at this table, Gran and

I. Always the two of us when I was young. I sighed in the sadness of the moment, feeling the memory across the years.

'I think we should go somewhere else before we get into any of this.' Angel addressed Grizelle. 'Given what happened earlier, I think we need more protection before we speak of this.' The other woman nodded.

I was still trying to catch up with all the evening's revelations.

As I looked from one to the other, it was as if the kitchen suddenly exploded. Like a bomb had gone off and every window shattered into a hundred million pieces. As I stood, with no time to cover my eyes or my face, I could see tiny slivers of glass travel through the air. I could feel the draft from the glass passing me by. I blinked and was looking at the ladies for a reaction. I knew my mouth was forming words slower than my mind was formulating them. I had no time to speak. Again there was that feeling of disassociation from my body as it stood there in the middle of the kitchen, with glass hanging in the air like mist.

Neither Angel nor Grizelle had made a move to cover their faces. Nor did they make a sound. The church bells rang and broke the spell for me.

12

I had crouched down, instinctively covering my head with my hands, letting out a shout of warning even though I knew it was too late. I had felt the glass screaming past my skin. Ready to gouge out patterns of pain.

Slowly, in the silence, I dropped my hands from my face and looked at Angel and Grizelle, expecting devastation. They were fine. They were whole. There was no broken glass. There were no shattered windows. It was all in my mind. Like the woman I'd seen at Gran's grave. Like the feeling of being pushed, or the monster in the fog or in my room. All in my mind. I was going crazy. Like my mum.

'Come now, come.' Grizelle grabbed me and gently hurried me out of the kitchen, blowing out the candle on the way. We stopped on the threshold and I noticed that the fog had appeared again, moving in silently to surround us.

Angel asked me for the keys and I robotically found them in my bag and handed them over. She locked the door quickly and I was guided towards her car. Grizelle jumped into a large dark estate car parked in front of the Beetle, and led the way back to the town.

Angel didn't say a word to me, just followed Grizelle's tail lights and drove round past the graveyard and then straight into the churchyard of St Mary's.

I had not expected that. If they had taken me straight to a mental hospital, I would have been less surprised. Of all the places in the town, we ended up at the church. I wanted to scream and not stop. What was going on? None of this made sense.

Angel and Grizelle helped me from the car and together we walked towards the church. We didn't say a word. Angel pulled my keys from her pocket and, after a couple of attempts, unlocked the door. *My gran had a key for the church! This was mad.*

We walked inside and the intermittent light as clouds danced in front of the moon guided us down the aisle towards the altar. The high stained glass windows lit up the ornately-carved interior, but it was still dark. Saintly statue shadows smiled down at us. Empty pews stood ready for whatever we would do. In front of the altar, Angel pulled over three high, wooden-backed, leather-seated chairs. I sat down. Angel stood behind me holding my head, one hand on my forehead, the other at the back of head. Grizelle held both of my hands and was the first to break the silence.

'Kirsty, you are okay. You didn't imagine it. We felt the glass. It wasn't your mind playing tricks. It was something much deeper.'

I was shocked. I hadn't told them anything about the glass. *How did she know?* I wanted to go home. Back to London. I had no business here. This was too crazy for me. I didn't trust myself to make any coherent words; I wanted to cry, scream or vomit. I was shaking.

Angel told me to keep my eyes closed and focus on my breathing. She told me to breathe in and out slowly as she counted. At the same time there was a sense, a feeling of comfort coming into my head. I'd had Reiki years before, and this was a similar sensation. Like a warmth, a tingle spreading throughout my body.

I could also feel something like that from Grizelle. A vibration, a stillness supporting me in the silence. She was quiet, with her eyes closed. The only sound was Angel counting my breaths. She told me to imagine that I had little roots coming down from my feet and digging themselves into the floor. To feel the roots push down gently and spread out, to feel the sensation of becoming anchored to the floor. To feel grounded, feel that the earth supported me from beneath. It held my weight, it looked after me. She called it Mother Earth, and there was something about the simplicity of her words which connected in me. She then guided me to bring green nurturing energy up from the earth, through these roots, and to feel that colour come up through my body into my heart.

Surprisingly, it worked and the panic and fear subsided, like a tingle of comfort filling my heart. I opened my eyes and looked closely at Grizelle. Eyes still closed, she was holding her hands out towards me as if in some sort of uplifting prayer. In a whisper she started to talk about the church. She told me that we were sitting at the centre of the cross which the church building made.

I looked around, as I hadn't realised the building was in the shape of a cross. It was too dark to see much but I had an idea in my head that she was right. We sat in its heart, the strongest part of the church energy. She said quartz crystals were built into the altar and their healing calming energy beamed out to congregations.

I peeked around as she spoke, still focusing on my breathing and Angel's hands on my head. After another few minutes she released me and sat down, holding her hands towards me in the same way as Grizelle. It felt like the rays from the sun or a fire. Warm and comforting, and I felt a little better; definitely calmer.

The whole episode at the house seemed less intense somehow. Perhaps it had been all the adrenalin and I'd imagined it. *But how had Grizelle known about the glass?* I looked at her and she opened her eyes.

'Feeling better now? This is the most protected place in the town. It's the perfect place to tell you a little more about our work with your gran.' I nodded and she carried on. 'This is a very sacred space. I do not use that term lightly. For generations our families have worshipped in this church. We have used our light to counteract the darkness. But these are challenging times. We live in a time of change, of what may look like progress to many, but to us – the light workers – it is a time to spread more love to other people and the planet. '

'What do you mean, Grizelle? What exactly did you do with my granny?' I was confused and a bit abrupt. I knew I didn't sound very polite but I was frustrated, tired and lonely, and still feeling so bad about Granny's death. 'I really don't know what you mean about lightness and darkness. And what happened at the cottage? How was the March Stone moved? Tell me, please tell me what you know.'

Grizelle didn't appear put out at my tone. 'For the moment, I can appreciate that you are finding this all very confusing, and I know that you are frustrated, but it will all become clearer soon. This is the way it has to be. You have to find your own way to understand this. Your gran will have left you some information which will help. We are helpers, your family are the Guardians. We do not know what you know…'

'Grizelle, I know nothing. Nothing. Granny hasn't left me anything… or at least, not with the solicitor. There might be something in the cottage but I haven't had time to look. You're really scaring me now…' I could feel the sobs and tears coming through, and knew they probably couldn't understand me. I hated crying in front of people like this. I cleared my throat and decided I'd had enough.

'If you can't or won't tell me what this is all about, then don't. I am leaving after the weekend and I really don't care. I've stumbled into something toxic, and I have had more than enough strange things happen to me for a lifetime. I'm leaving.'

Angel leaned over and held me close. Something about the human touch was so comforting and I struggled not to cry again.

'I have made up my mind… I'm going home… I'll sort out the cottage and clear Gran's things… This is all too much.'

'It's okay,' said Angel. 'Leave it all for now. It's a hard time, but Grizelle isn't trying to be difficult with you. You need to take care of yourself. We know you have your personal grief, but your gran was part of a much bigger plan, and we know dark days are coming. She wanted to help more and that's why she decided it was time to go. We know you think this is all crazy and we probably seem insane to you, but can we ask you for just one thing? Please?' Angel's bright blue eyes pleaded with me.

'Go within, Kirsty. Do what your heart says to do. Don't run away from fear of not knowing or understanding something. Where will that get you in your life? The last few days have been hard because there are things happening in the town. Things that are powerful and not for the greater good. I know that you will do what is right in the end. We have faith in you.'

It was like they were speaking in another language. I felt anger bubble up and was about to shout back, but something about what she said or the way she said it changed me. Something told me to tell them about the experience outside the pub, at the B&B, in the graveyard. I felt it was okay to confide in them. In spite, or perhaps because of what had happened with them, I knew from somewhere inside me that they would understand. That they would not think me mad.

When I'd finished, Angel and Grizelle shared another one of their looks. I knew that they believed me, but that there was something worrying them.

'What are you thinking? What's going to happen? What happened at the cottage and with the stone? Please tell me what you know.'

Angel answered for them both. 'We don't know for sure, but I can only tell you what we do know. You might have realised by now that we worked with your gran and that we all have "gifts" of intuition, or second sight, call it what you like. We've always had a strong sense of knowing about life – for ourselves, other people, and the town, and I suppose the world. But for the first time none of us could see the future. None of us. This has never happened before. We have instinctively worked in threes, probably for generations… three women together, especially from different age groups, is a powerful combination. We all knew that we were here in this town to maintain some sort of "reite". There is no word for it in English – it's like keeping an arrangement, keeping everything level.'

She had asked me to go within and I instinctively knew that what she was saying was the truth. As I shivered and looked around the dark, shadowed church, something told me that my poor mum had heard the same thing, and it had sent her running into the stormy night.

For the first time in years I felt Mum with me. I could feel her draw close to me, I felt her tears and pain of the past, and I felt her faith in me. I didn't know why but I sensed I was doing this for her. As I felt peace in my heart, I could feel my gran coming close, and something more. In the dark of the church, it was as if the place was sending peace and power up through my feet and into my body.

'We feel that something darker, unpleasant, unholy is coming close. We think that's what moved the March Stone at the house. Those stones were put in place a long time ago. There might be more information in the library or the museum. Without your gran here, darkness is visiting the town.'

'Unholy? Do you really think so? It seems a bit extreme?' I'd had such strange experiences over the last few days that this was almost starting to feel normal. 'Angel, why did you throw salt around the cottage?'

'It's an old way of protecting a house from evil and the darkness. I… knew the stone was in danger and we had to get it back into position before anything else happened.'

'What about the star in the circle that you drew? What did that do?'

'Again it's about protection, and it was good that the three of us were together in the kitchen… Three women of different generations… a very powerful combination of protective energies. The Divine Feminine.'

They both exchanged an all-knowing look and I was on the outside looking in; it was the way I'd felt all my life, really. I didn't understand any of this but I didn't want to ask much either. I wasn't sure why, but I had the feeling I wasn't going to get much more out of them.

Unsurprisingly, Angel and Grizelle seemed to sense the change in me, and both stood up as an ending to the conversation. Without words, we left and locked the church. Grizelle hugged us both then drove off into the fog which had surrounded the building, dampening down the light. Angel and I left her car at the church, and slipped through the gate around the path into the courtyard, and went upstairs to her flat.

Within a few minutes she had worked her magic and heat and light filled the nooks and crannies of her home. I had a quick shower, and by the time I returned to the main lounge she'd put hot soup, sandwiches, cakes and tea on the low coffee table. I was suddenly ravenous and devoured everything, then said goodnight and went to bed.

Angel suggested I take the dragon's head crystal to bed with me, and although it was heavy and an odd shape, it felt good to have it close to me on the pillow.

It was so dark and foggy outside that I had no idea what time it was, but I was exhausted. In answer to my unspoken question, the church clock struck ten times. I snuggled further under the duvet, my mind and thoughts filled with images of my mother. I felt such compassion for her as I knew how easily I could have descended into a breakdown. And some part of me realised that she had been with me – her and Gran – over the last few days. That thought felt good, and I slipped into sleep.

Sometime during the night, I heard the church bells. I was dreaming that I was a nun or monk years ago. I sensed my bare feet and long gown, holding it up as I hurried to prayer in the church. I was cold and shivering, and realised that I'd actually risen from bed and was kneeling on the floor. It had been ages since I'd walked about in my sleep.

I was disorientated, and for those first few minutes I didn't know where I was, where the bed was, or I suppose who or what I was. I slept again, waking with dreams of dragons and crystals and caves a couple of times during the night, but always returning to sleep.

13

The sound of church bells woke me early, and I made myself a mug of tea and jumped back into my warm bed. I heard Angel pottering around the kitchen before she left about eight o'clock, and then I dozed again for an hour or so. When I woke, I realised that I had some options – as well as some work to do.

Did I really want to go back to London? I now had a house and some money coming to me. Could I stay here in the town and make a new life for myself? It would be good to get out of the rat race. To do something completely different. My work was interesting but it felt pointless, an endless shuffling of paper.

And did I really want Derek? That relationship was like so much of my life, a habit I'd fallen into. When was the last time I had done anything exciting? Our annual two week holiday in France was hardly challenging, was it? Despite all the fears and worries and, of course, the pain of the recent weeks, I had to be honest and admit that there was something in me that had felt awakened by all my experiences. I wasn't sure if that was all good or all bad, but at least it was different. And there was a little feeling inside that told me that everything would turn out well.

I wanted to get back to Gran's house to check if there was anything left for me. Something personal; something that would explain more about my family and what my ancestors had done. Perhaps something that would tell me how or why the March Stone had been moved, and what was under it. Angel and Grizelle seemed to be worried, so there must be something wrong, and they had both talked about Gran choosing to die. There had to be more to it, but I had no idea what that would be.

To be honest, part of me was scared about going to Gran's house on my own, but I didn't want to ask Angel to take time off again and I knew I had to face it sometime. Was there really anything to be scared of? Rationally, I knew my gran would never have hurt me, nor would my mother, so why would they want to harm me in death? They couldn't and wouldn't; I knew that deep inside.

But as I left the house and ran into *Angel's Cakes*, I still felt uneasy and anxious. Angel was busy with customers so I gestured to her that I was heading back to Gran's and she gave me a thumbs up, which I took to mean she knew what I was doing and approved.

I cut through Dead Man's Lane at the side of the cemetery, past the new school, and found myself back at Granny's door. I wanted to avoid the March Stone, but I needed to know more about what had happened yesterday.

The stone sat solidly in the frozen earth, the markings on it the same as I remembered from childhood play. Patterns of spirals and elaborate swirls all over and along the top, little holes as if cups had been cut out of the stone. All exactly the same.

The local archaeology club had taken rubbings from all the Stones years before, and said they'd been made by Stone Age man, but I thought that unlikely. I mean, how could a caveman have cut such beautiful intricate patterns into solid stone? What tools would they have used to do that? And why would they have put thirteen almost identical stones all around the town?

I knew that garden so well, and I knew no-one would have been able to dig around the stone without machinery. It was a Scottish winter. Who could turn over soil in those conditions? As strange as it seemed, I wondered if the stone could have been pushed from underneath. Was that even possible? How could that happen, and who could have done it? Or should that be *what* could have done it?

I gave myself a shake. All the spooky chat from Angel and Grizelle was starting to sound reasonable to me. I decided that there would be a rational explanation, perhaps the quarry expansion had done something to the ground. A mini earthquake? Yes, that sounded more likely. With that thought, I headed over to the house.

It felt quieter and softer than the previous night. It was as if the house welcomed me in. I decided to start in the lounge and worked my way back to the kitchen, leaving searching Gran's bedroom until last. *But if she was going to leave me something, would it more likely to be in my bedroom or hers?* I just wished I could talk to her, and with that thought, fresh tears flowed. The house was so strangely quiet and I realised that I had rarely been in it on my own.

I took the opportunity to clear out some old magazines and newspapers, and soon filled the recycling bin. I found beeswax polish and a duster under the sink and cleaned the furniture, then I brushed the rug and carpet, but I left the circle and star of salt on the floor and on the window sills and doorways. In a strange way I understood that it was for protection, from what I didn't dare contemplate. I didn't want the noise of the vacuum cleaner to intrude, and I found cleaning and clearing strangely therapeutic.

Once or twice I thought I heard Gran call for me, and although I was crying it was comforting as if she really was just in the next room.

However, I didn't find anything out of the ordinary; I wasn't sure exactly what I was looking for. Perhaps a letter addressed to me? Or was that too simple and obvious? My mind reran the last few days. *What had she left me? What did she pass on to me?*

I climbed the stairs and opened the door to what had been my mother's bedroom. It was empty apart from a wooden bed frame without a mattress, and an empty wardrobe.

I crossed the landing and opened the door to my childhood; such a long time since I'd slept there. The walls had been cleared of my old posters and redecorated, but the memory of them hung around. Faded soft toys were displayed on the window sill, a dried-up starfish sat in a plastic container from a long forgotten visit to a seaside, alongside my collection of old stones and bits of glass I'd thought were gem stones. With a sad heart I sat on the unmade bed and cried again for all that I had lost. For the child I had been and the woman I had become. I was lost.

There was nothing of my gran in this room. I knew I had looked everywhere I could think of. The only place left was her bedroom, and with a shock I realised that I hadn't been inside it in years.

I took a deep breath and tried to stay strong. I thought back to the previous night and that feeling I'd had in the church when Angel and Grizelle sat around me with their hands up sending some sort of good feeling to me. Perhaps it was also just taking a deep breath, but somehow I found the courage to open the door.

As it swung open, I imagined that I might see Granny standing by her window or by her bed, but she wasn't there. Instead, I saw a neat and tidy room. Floral wallpaper and pale green carpet, with matching velvet curtains and sparkling white nets, diffusing the light. It was as if she'd stepped out for a moment. And I sat down on the bed trying not to cry again. This was all so painful. I really didn't want to stay long in this room. I knew I'd be leaving it a while before I'd come back in.

I looked in the drawers in the cabinets beside her bed, but there wasn't much in them. A couple of books, a sapphire brooch she often wore, her reading glasses. I had a quick look at her book shelves and even under her pillows, but nothing looked unusual and I had a feeling that I wouldn't find a letter there.

I opened the wardrobe door, and there on the top shelf were the rest of my childhood toys. My angels, my little unicorn ornaments, my collection of cherub snow globes. All sitting waiting for me to discover them again. I couldn't close the door on them, and instead took them through to the sitting room and sat down on the couch with them in my arms. I leaned back and closed my eyes, feeling the memories flooding in and my gran and mum coming closer. Like a light in the darkness of my thoughts. I had no tears left to cry, but like the experience at the graveyard, I felt them both. As though they were beside me. I sensed them and I sobbed, 'Gran, I'm so sorry.'

I felt like a huge light explode in my eyes and in my heart. I heard or felt her say she was proud of me, to dry my tears, that I was her special girl. If it was my imagination, I didn't care. It was what I most wanted and needed to hear.

The sound of the church bells striking three interrupted my daydreams. I hadn't realised I had been in the house so long. It was time to leave and head back to town to see Angel and grab a late lunch. There was nothing here to help me; at least, nothing obvious.

I talked to Gran in my head all the way back to town. 'Please help me. Please help me, and make it obvious.'

14

I saw a young girl handing out leaflets outside the church. In her orange cagoule and bobbly hat, she seemed bright in the miserable grey drizzle, and the wild wind threatened to whip the papers from her gloved hand. I took a damp leaflet from her and shivered as I walked past the railings, not hanging about to admire the architecture. From my experience last night, I now knew the church was so much more than that.

When I pushed open the glass doors into *Angel's Cakes* that wonderful aroma of coffee and toasted bread, and the sound of people laughing and chatting, welcomed me in. I saw that Angel had taped one of the multi-coloured leaflets to her counter, and I narrowed my eyes to read it as I waited to be served.

It was an invitation to a public meeting that evening in the Memorial Hall. That's where all the town meetings took place, and this one was being held by the Town Council. Council officials, according to the leaflet, would be there to discuss the planning decision on the quarry extension, and representatives of the quarry owner would also be in attendance to answer any questions. This was an opportunity for the town to hear all about the plans, and to voice any objections.

Angel appeared from the back shop, red-cheeked and perspiring, which was hardly surprising as she carried a huge cauldron of bubbling hot soup. She broke into a cheeky grin when she saw me, and said she was planning to take a break and would join me. I gave her my order and found a seat, and five minutes later we were sitting together eating toasted cheese sandwiches and drinking coffee.

'How did it go at your gran's? And how are you feeling now after last night? Did you sleep okay?' she asked. 'Did you find anything?'

She was obviously concerned and really interested in what had happened. So I explained that I hadn't found anything, and although I'd felt upset and found it difficult, I'd been able to look through the cottage, including Gran's room.

She rubbed my arm in acknowledgement of my achievement. 'How brave of you. I know I found it hard to clear out my parents' things after they had gone. It's not easy for anyone at these times. It must have been difficult, but I bet you're glad you've done it.'

And she was right. I was pleased that I'd been able to go round on my own. As silly as it seems, I was proud of myself for doing it. I had always had a fear of death. I suppose you wouldn't need to be a psychologist to understand that, having lost my parents so young. My gran always used to say that people held on too long to their childhood experiences. She would say that it's thoughts of the past that make us sad in the present so that we worry about the future rather than enjoying what we have.

I smiled. It was funny, it was almost as if she was in my head at that moment, with all her wisdom and optimism.

'So did you hear about the public meeting tonight?' Angel was chattering again. 'Grizelle and I are going, will you join us? We have the feeling that it's important we all attend. Sometimes these things can go a bit over the top... heightened emotions and all that, and people can say and do things that can upset others.'

'Will you do that thing you did with me last night?' I replied shyly. 'You know… with the way you held your hands?'

Angel laughed. 'Well, we might not have to. I'll take some smoky quartz crystals with me, as that helps transmute negativity. You might laugh, but your gran got the builders to put smoky and pink quartz into the walls of the Memorial Hall when they were renovating it last year!'

She giggled and looked really pleased with herself, and as much as I didn't know that much about crystals, I had to smile at the thought of my wee gran asking big burly builders to pop crystals behind walls. I wish I'd seen that.

I told Angel that I planned to go and see the doctor to ask more about Gran, but that I really wanted to talk to her about what had happened the night before, especially about the movement of the March Stone, and the visions I'd seen of the messed kitchen and then the explosion. She suggested I go round to the doctor's surgery and ask to see him, rather than telephone for an appointment, and that she and I would talk later.

Outside, the drizzle had turned into sleet which blew horizontally in bursts into my face. I was freezing and wet to the core by the time I pushed against the wind and got to the surgery. It was still on the same site I remembered at the back of the train station, uphill from *The Three Keys*. Now, though, it was in a purpose-built, low building, housing a pharmacy and some clinics, rather than the old draughty house I remembered from childhood visits.

The wide glass door opened automatically and I felt as if I flew into the brightly-lit foyer, bringing in icy wind to the harassed and unhappy-looking receptionist. When I asked if it was possible to see the doctor for a few minutes, I knew that she was going to say no. But at that moment a blond woman around my age came out of one of the offices and called my name.

It took me a few moments to recognise that it was one of my closest friends from primary school.

'Carole,' I said, genuinely pleased to see a familiar face. 'I haven't seen you for years. How on earth did you recognise me?'

'You haven't changed a bit, Kirsty!' She laughed. 'And I sort of expected to see you after hearing about your gran. I'm so sorry. She was such a great character.'

She was sympathetic, and when I asked if it was possible to have a brief word with the doctor, Carole offered to try to catch him before he left for the evening.

Within a few minutes she was back, then buzzed me through a security door and pointed to a door further along the sage green corridor. I knocked quietly and entered hesitantly when a voice called me in.

I had expected old Dr McLeod, but this was a much younger man. Obviously used to the surprised reaction, he laughed and explained that he had taken over from his father three years before. After we shook hand, he professionally rearranged his features into a sombre expression as he said he was sorry for my loss.

'Dr McLeod, I'm not sure exactly why I'm here. I suppose I was hoping for some answers,' I began. 'I understand that my gran was coming to see you and that she was ill. And that you found her?'

His eyebrows rose in surprise. 'Please sit down and I'll do what I can to help. I wish all my patients were as fit and healthy as your gran was. I wasn't treating Kirsten for anything. As far as I knew, she was in fine fettle for a woman of her age… just a couple of aches and pains which she didn't want help with.' He gave a wry smile. 'She said she had something for that.'

I was shocked. 'But, Doctor, if you weren't treating her for anything, why were you at the house? What exactly happened to her?'

This didn't make any sense to me, and I could feel a pulse beating fiercely somewhere at the front of my brain, blocking out the desk, the room, noises of the telephone from reception. I was focused on him. I saw him lick his lips, then bow his head slightly as if working out what to say or how best to say it.

'I feel I have to tell you what I know. She came in a couple of months ago for an annual check-up. She said she was feeling a bit more tired than normal, but said she knew it wouldn't last forever. Something was bothering her, but she said it was all under control so I didn't push it.

'Then last week she called in and asked one of our receptionists – Carole, I think – to book me in for a home visit. She didn't say what it was about and I can only assume that she wasn't feeling well. It was so unusual for her to ask that I felt it was important, so I decided to go out in the morning before the surgery opened. I got to the cottage before nine, and saw that she had left the door slightly open. There was a note pinned to it asking me to go in, and that she was in the bedroom.'

He swallowed and paused briefly before continuing. 'It was such a lovely day. I remember admiring the garden, such a beautiful view, the best in the town, I'm sure, and there was a bright rainbow hanging over the Falls across the valley. It was magical, so much quieter than in the town. I'd love to live there. You are very lucky, you know. Anyway, I went into the cottage calling for her, but I suppose as medics we get a sixth sense for these things. I knew she had passed away before I got into the bedroom.

'She looked so peaceful lying in her bed, and there was a note for me on the bedside table with your number to call and to let the Jacks' and Douglas the solicitor know, as she had made arrangements with them.' He shrugged slightly. 'So I made all the calls and they took over.'

I felt a tear roll down my cheek as he described finding Granny. What a woman she was, to call and arrange for the doctor to come in and find her, rather than a friend or neighbour. That took some courage and trust.

I struggled to compose myself as the doctor went on to explain that even though Gran's death had been unexpected, they had felt that given her age and the fact that she had arranged the home visit, she must have felt ill. A post mortem had been carried out, as the law dictates for sudden deaths, but that nothing obvious had shown up. As a result, a death certificate stating 'natural causes' had been issued to allow the funeral to take place.

It all made such perfect sense. My only sadness was that Gran had passed away on her own, and that I hadn't been able to be with her and hold her hand as she slipped away. The Doctor said he believed that her passing had been peaceful, probably in her sleep, and I liked that she might have been dreaming of happy times as she left this world.

I couldn't wait to tell Angel and Grizelle, but then realised that it wouldn't be news to them. They had sensed it, or Gran had told them somehow.

When I caught him glancing at his watch, I stood and thanked Dr McLeod for his time. He looked tired, and I guessed he wanted to be on his way home. I looked out for Carole as I left but she wasn't around for me to thank her again. Instead, I smiled at the receptionist, and she surprised me by smiling back. Maybe she'd had a hard day as well. It couldn't be easy being surrounded by sick people every day, all needing to see the doctor. I couldn't do a job like that.

It was cold outside, and the rain was bouncing off the road like someone had left a tap running and a bath had overflowed. A bath of very cold water, though, and I had to dodge in and out of grey puddles to try to avoid the worst and the splashes from cars and buses.

I was soaked to the skin by the time I got back to the flat, and I quickly lit the stove and changed into dry clothes. Switching the kettle on to make a hot drink, I found the book Angel had given me on my first night. Sitting on her big comfy sofa, I felt welcomed by the flames but couldn't read a word. Tears blinded my vision at the thought of my wonderful, selfless gran, who would have done anything to help anyone, passing away into death on her own. What I would have given to be able to rewind and be there with her, holding her hand, telling her I loved her. My heart felt dragged down with sadness.

But the moment passed, and instead in my mind I saw a picture of my gran in her garden. She looked the same as always, but softer somehow, younger, smiling at me, laughing, so real that I could have put out my hand and touched her face.

I suddenly remembered something she had told me years ago when I was young and we had been talking about death. She said that no-one dies on their own. When we die, our families come back from heaven and take us with them. She told me that when her grandfather was dying, he said he could see his own mother and father waiting for him, and that there was light all around them, so he wasn't scared to go with them.

That memory gave me comfort. It was as if Granny had popped it into my head to remind me. And then the vision faded, and I wiped my eyes with the back of my hand.

I heard Angel come in and go straight into the kitchen, and within a few minutes I could smell garlic and other delights, and my tummy rumbled in anticipation.

'Are you still okay to come to the meeting tonight?' she asked. 'I thought we could eat and then go over a bit earlier. I'm feeling it might get a bit, you know, mad when the townspeople hear about the plans.'

'Has planning permission actually been granted yet?' I asked.

'We know it has, but that's all unofficial and I doubt that they will announce it tonight, not in front of the whole town. I think they'll release it on their website soon. I think tonight is about looking like they care.' I was surprised to hear Angel talk so dismissively; she had always seemed so calm and upbeat.

'Maybe not. Let's stay positive,' I said. 'You never know, maybe the angels will be looking after us!'

Angel's eyes moistened with tears. 'They always do,' she said, wiping a hand across her eyes, 'but sometimes we don't realise when things are for the best.'

15

Atter dinner the heavy rain had eased, and although damp and a little foggy we walked to the top of the High Street and the grand pilloried entrance to the Memorial Hall, a large Victorian ornately decorated meeting place. It had been built when the town was a centre of commerce in the area. The main hall was stunning, with dark wood panelling and a patterned marble floor. Glass and gold chandeliers dazzled high above our heads.

I wondered where Gran had placed the quartz, and for a moment felt a tug towards her, a real connection to her fun side. I could see her doing it here in this building, with a cheeky glint in her eye. How could anyone have resisted her? And she would most likely have known the families of the builders, in any case. I was sure she would have told them so.

I saw Grizelle come in and take a seat at the back of the room to the left of the doorway; Angel and I sat across from her on the right hand side. Seats were filling up quickly and I realised that Grizelle and Angel had decided to do what they had done to me in the church, healing or hold the energies, I think one of them had said.

Within a few minutes the hall was filled with townsfolk. I recognised many as neighbours and friends of my gran, and people who ran the local shops and businesses. In a small town you see the same people all the time, so even though you might not speak to them, you still know who they are.

After a few minutes of waiting, people were getting restless, fidgeting and crossing and uncrossing their legs, and shuffling around on their seats. There were lots of loud coughs given it was winter, noisy chat, and the smell of wet wool filled the room.

About ten minutes later the council officials and representatives from the quarry and town council came in and took their places on a long table at the far end of the room. It was on a slightly raised platform, so I could see them all easily. I wasn't sure who was who; they all looked the same, middle-aged men in suits, shirts and ties, all seemingly very friendly with each other. I had a sense that they were pleased with themselves and I knew my gran wouldn't have approved.

One of the men introduced himself as the Deputy Head of Planning, then he introduced all the others. The audience was silent but I could sense the mood wasn't good. People sat with crossed arms and frowns, waiting for a chance to speak. One of the men from the quarry company got to his feet and gave a presentation showing a tiny map which I certainly couldn't see from the back of the room. People started to heckle him, and within minutes people were shouting out and talking over each other. The planning official tried to keep order by telling people to wait and allow the presenter to finish.

This seemed to infuriate the townspeople further, and a lot of them, especially those towards the back, jumped to their feet shouting and gesturing angrily. The local press photographer was running around taking photos, which only seemed to result in winding people up even more.

I heard a roar and a loud bang as the ornate double doors crashed open and a large crowd pushed their way into the meeting. The two old, uniformed security guards struggled to keep them back, not physically fit or emotionally ready for such an onslaught. The group forced their way in and rushed to the staged area, shouting and waving banners. Chairs were knocked flying, people were pushing against each other, and the whole room descended into chaos.

I joined Angel and Grizelle who had quickly moved against the back wall but still seemed to be praying or meditating in some way. They were the only ones showing serenity, as if the conflict and confusion was happening a million miles away.

I didn't recognise anyone in this new group, but amidst the chaos I noticed that they seemed well organised. Most of them headed to the front of the hall towards the officials on the small stage, while others made for the three other exit doors and stood with their placards and banners. Their actions were intimidating, and people seemed scared as well as angry.

From their knitted woollen ponchos and sweaters, and multi-coloured dreadlocked hair, they looked like what I'd expected environmental activists to look like. I'd always assumed those types to be peaceful, but this group was aggressive and, from what I could see, violent and intent on causing problems. More chairs were overturned, and I saw a couple of the environmentalists lift them up and smash them against the wall. Papers, pamphlets, and the presentation equipment were strewn across the floor.

I had a sudden thought that these protesters weren't in the town to spread a message of environmentalism, they were in the town to cause problems. Everyone was roaring at each other. I saw church elders and senior members of the town pushing and pulling each other, so angry that they were spitting fury. Punches were being thrown, people were rolling around on the floor trying to hit each other. Men and women of all ages, and all seeming to be possessed by the same angry, aggressive spirit. I had never seen anything like it. It was bedlam. Chaos. Like a bar-room brawl.

The three of us, along with several other ladies and a couple of elderly gentlemen, were pushed back against the doorway and the force of destruction propelled us into the main hallway. In the distance we could hear a police siren, and we looked at each other in horror. The two elderly security guards, shaken and ashen-faced, ran out to the street to wait for the police. They were followed out by several of the council officials, looking equally pale and scared. By this time, the environmentalists had taken over the raised area and were still shouting.

Angel and Grizelle seemed to be the only ones apparently unmoved by the experience. We walked backwards out of the building and, without discussion, headed towards Angel's flat. Behind us we heard the noise reduce, probably as people realised that the police were on their way.

'What's happened to this town?' I asked, still in shock at seeing people I'd grown up with and respected fighting and shouting with each other. I couldn't believe how quickly the meeting had turned into mob rule.

'What is that group doing in the town? I asked. 'I don't know any of them. Where are they from? It was like "rent-a-mob"! I thought environmentalists were supposed to be peaceful. Those guys were like something you see on the TV outside global political summits… and how quick to anger were some of the townspeople?' I knew I was rambling nervously, but I couldn't seem to help myself, my mind was a jumble of thoughts and questions. 'Even the business people were going crazy. We didn't get a chance to hear what was happening or when they would announce the results of the planning application. Did either of you hear the detail of how close the quarry would get to town? After all, Gran's cottage is close as well.'

'I heard someone say that there would be news tomorrow,' Angel replied calmly. 'It will probably go out on their website. Events like tonight play into the hands of the politicians and council. They'll say that they can make better, less emotional decisions for the good of the town, because we can't be trusted.'

Grizelle, walking quietly in the middle of us, suddenly stopped and grasped us both by the arm. 'I have an anxious feeling,' she said quietly. 'Angel, would you be okay if we all went to your place? I feel we have to have a ceremony to clear these stuck energies over the town. Something just doesn't feel right.'

As she finished, I looked around me and noticed that the fog had once again descended, filling the usually clear air with an opaque, other-worldly tinge. Despite my warm waterproof clothing, I shivered.

Within a few minutes we reached the courtyard, but instead of climbing to the warm, well-lit flat, Angel and Grizelle stepped over to the pyramid structure, lifted one end of the brushwood covering and herded me inside. Angel tapped some lamps and I realised that they were battery-operated and shone some light onto the brass-piped pyramid inside. As we bent inside the structure and sat down, I noticed coloured crystals hanging down from the centre point five feet or so above our heads. There would have been space for maybe ten people inside. It was like a Native American wigwam, similar to a red one I'd owned as a child.

I breathed in an aroma of earth and pine, added to the fragrance of sandalwood incense as Angel burned a stick in a small holder at her feet. She lovingly touched and re-arranged small crystals in the middle of where we sat, as if welcoming them to our party.

Then Grizelle took charge, sitting across from Angel and me, breathing in and out deeply. We sat for a few minutes in silence whilst my eyes adjusted to the dullness, but my mind was racing. There was something so bizarre about the last few days and yet it all felt very familiar, normal even. It was as if some deep part of my DNA knew all of this already; perhaps that's why I had started to accept it.

Grizelle spoke in her usual deep tones, and I immediately closed my eyes without bidding.

'Mother Earth and Father Sky,' she said, 'please send love and light into the heart of everyone involved tonight. Please help those struggling with fear to find a new way to express themselves and move into the light of love. Please help all of us to accept all aspects of ourselves; the shadow and the light; the masculine and the feminine; the mind and the heart. Please send light to the town and help us with healing anything which hurts us, and let us turn that into love. For the highest good of all concerned. Amen.'

They both sat for another few minutes with eyes closed, as I nervously glanced around the pyramid. We couldn't see the church, but I had a sense that its light had dimmed in the foggy night, and I had a horrible feeling of fear that something nasty was coming, but I didn't know what.

When I looked back, Angel and Grizelle were watching me intently, and Grizelle asked what I was feeling. I tried to shakily laugh off my thoughts and feelings of dread, and instead asked about what she had said.

'Was that a prayer or a meditation, Grizelle?'

'Both,' she replied. 'We do what we do to help people as they struggle with life and emotion. It is not for us to judge. We've all been in a place of fear, and we all know how easy it is to react when we feel afraid. People are good at heart, but sometimes they forget that.'

I didn't want to disagree with her, given the crazy night we'd just experienced, so instead I asked another question.

'What do you think is happening here? Angel said you knew lots about the history of the town. Is there a legend about the danger of the March Stones being moved? Do we even know who put them there, or why? And do you know what the markings on them mean? The spirals and the holes at the top.'

I knew that all the March Stones had similar, if not identical, symbols on them, but that only our stone had the holes along the top; cups, I think they had been called. Personally, I thought it was ancient vandals, bored with life, who had scratched away in the surface of the stones not knowing that hundreds of years later people would want to know more. To me, it was ancient history and not that interesting. But something told me that Grizelle might have been one of the volunteers at the museum and was taking it seriously.

'There is a legend, yes,' she told me. 'I don't believe it has been written down, but if there is anything, I think you might find the museum or the library of interest. Your gran and I would meet there often to look through their archives. The markings are similar to those made by Stone Age man in other sites throughout the West of Scotland and Ireland. The spiral shape is shown a lot in early Celtic art, and relates to energy, the sun, the earth, elements and eternity. The cups were cut into the stone to signify water.

'Your gran believed that the March Stones were standing stones, put there by Stone Age man, perhaps by Druids. After all, there was a Druid temple uncovered in Glasgow only 25 miles from here, along the River Clyde. We know they held the earth in reverence, so is it too much of a stretch of the imagination to believe that this was one of their sacred sites?'

'I didn't know there was a Druid temple in Glasgow.' I was intrigued. 'Where is it?'

'On the boulevard heading west. I read that it was covered over before the Second World War to make a roadway, would you believe? But I think the energy of the place still exists. Just like here, and we know that Christianity often "borrowed" the sites and ceremonies of earlier times, like pagan festivals.'

'So there are other sites which have the same types of stones?' I asked.

'Probably hundreds, if not thousands of sites,' she said, 'but your gran believed that there was something especially important about our stones. Particularly because of the way they surrounded the church site. She believed that there was something special here which needed protection. Perhaps that's too harsh a word for you and conjures up fear? For us, it's about safeguarding and maintaining balance. Think of that instead.

'There was a settlement of people on this site from early Stone Age, as far as we know from the artefacts found locally,' she continued. 'We also know that the Romans found the town to be of strategic importance to their domination of the region.'

'Hold on,' I interrupted. 'I thought the Romans didn't get into Scotland. Isn't that what Hadrian's Wall was all about, to keep Scots out of Roman Britain?'

She smiled. 'It's true that the Romans did build Hadrian's Wall to protect the rest of Britain, but there were many attempts to colonise the North. We know that there was a Roman garrison here in the town. It is said that they tried to move the old March Stones, and that's when monsters from beneath were awakened to unleash hell on earth. The Romans retreated south and built the wall for protection from the Picts, and the other ancient tribes and their supernatural helpers.'

'Supernatural? What do you mean?' This was too strange to believe. I was sure Grizelle was playing a trick on me, or else was unhinged. What else could there be?

'I'm sure you will find some really interesting information in the museum and the library. There are some copies of ancient manuscripts from the Romans about a great defeat which happened here at their garrison. They lost many men in a single night, or to be more accurate, many men "disappeared" in a single night. No record of a battle exists in any of the literature, though. So we surmise that there was an incident and the word "supernatural" appears in the literature.

It's not me trying to trick you or losing my mind, I can assure you of that.'

It was as if she had read my mind. I took a deep breath and asked again about the markings on the stones.

'Could they help with this? Whatever *this* is. I know you said you had a horrible feeling. Can you tell me more about things?'

A cold, sharp wind blew against the pyramid and we all jumped in fright.

'Let's go up to the flat and have a hot drink,' Angel suggested.

As we climbed the stairs, I couldn't help looking behind me into the grey swirls of fog. Grizelle and Angel kept talking about protection or safeguarding, but it all sounded the same to me. Despite their words, I really felt like we were being watched.

16

Upstairs, it took Angel only a few minutes to again work her magic and soon we were sitting across from the dancing firelight, with warm drinks and cakes laid out on the low table in front of us. I could see only fog through the big window. As I'd imagined, the light from the church had indeed dimmed and it was hardly discernible through the foggy night.

Grizelle, sitting across from me, asked if it would be helpful for me to know more about her friendship with my gran. Keen to have something tangible to investigate or hold onto, I nodded encouragingly and sipped my hot tea. Despite everything, I still feared that there was some sort of insanity hovering close to me.

'Our families have been friends for generations,' she began, 'and your gran and I played together as children. Although she was a little older than me, our mothers were good friends. While still quite young, we were introduced to the other side of our families' lives, if you will. We were trained in the power of nature, and taught to accept that there is an innate intelligence in life.

'No-one has to tell a seed planted in the ground how to grow, and we see that acorns turn into oak trees, not birch or fir. We were shown by our mothers how beautiful life is and how all we need to thrive is all around us. Like your gran, I have never left this place. Why would I, when everything I need is all around me?'

'By the time we were teenagers, we understood herbs and plants and how to work with them to benefit others. Your gran also had some special gifts of helping people understand how to love and accept themselves. After all, isn't that what we all seek? Some might call it enlightenment, but for others it's called contentment. When we stop looking for something outside of ourselves, we come into our own. Your gran would help people with this. She called it "balance".'

Grizelle paused briefly to drink her tea, and I waited patiently for her to continue her story.

'As well as helping people, we knew we had another role. This town is such an important place, and many have recognised that over the years. We knew we were here to safeguard the March Stones. So many myths had grown up around the stones over the years. But more recently the townspeople had moved away from any sort of legend, and the Stones had become part of a tourist attraction along with the bands and the festivities. To be honest, that suited us all, as we felt it a smokescreen.

'Like your gran, I married young. To an accountant from Edinburgh. Gordon was a lovely man, but he didn't understand nor accept my need to be here. He was a very practical person and I think he found my beliefs a bit strange. We argued all the time. It really wasn't a happy marriage. Over time, I found it exhausting continually having to defend my beliefs. If I said I was going over to your gran's house for anything, his eyebrows would rise and he'd make a face of what looked like derision or contempt, or at least that's how I saw it.'

She shook her head slightly, as if trying to rid herself of the unhappy memories.

'It was a really horrible time my life. I lost my way. And all the time I pretended to everyone that things were good. The stress was terrible. But your gran knew and understood. She said he would come round in his own time, and she was a great support. I think I would have gone mad if she hadn't been there for me. You have to understand, we weren't doing anything bad, or even that strange by today's standards. We met and meditated; we worked with herbs and plants; we grew them at your gran's house.

'Oh, how I loved that garden.' She and Angel shared a smile. 'As soon as I stepped into the garden, I could feel my tension ooze away. It always felt magical to me. And then, of course, there was the March Stone. The thirteenth stone. We would sit at it for hours, feeling its energy of peace and protection. I believe that's what the symbols meant. Just think, they were carved thousands of years ago by people who wanted to leave a mark. They must have been important to them, and all that time later they were important to me and your gran, and to all our ancestors before us. Beneath the trees we could sit and feel strong and safe and, yes, protected.

'I know you are wondering from what? But I can't answer that. Your gran had to be the one to tell you, because your family had a special purpose. I can guess, but that's not the same as hearing it from Kirsten herself. I knew that woman so well, and I know that she had found a way to really help us....'

My thoughts took me back to the conversation with Angel the previous night. 'Why here, and why now?'

'Again, all I can tell you is that we all had a sense, a feeling, that things were changing, and are continuing to change here. We could feel a disaster coming towards us, but without our usual knowing of what that was. Personally, I believe it is connected to the quarry expansion. In my dreams I can hear the stones calling to me, to all of us, to prepare, to get strong, to be aware. What that means, though, I really don't know.'

She ran her hand through her hair in a gesture of tiredness or frustration, I wasn't sure which. 'Your gran and I had such a connection that I know she found a way to help, and I really, truly believe that she is helping us even now. For me, death is not the end, it's only the end of our current physical life. Death permits us to move into spirit, infinite, expansive, universally connected.'

She paused and gave me a sympathetic smile. 'Forgive me if this is hard to hear when you loved your grandmother as much as you did, but this is another beginning for her and for all of us. I know she will be helping the way she always has, but in a different and bigger way. Does this make any sense to you at all, Kirsty?'

I realised that I had tears on my face. I didn't know if it due to her words, her faith or a sadness inside me. I knew I could sense Gran and my mum moving closer to me. As if in answer, the lights and candles around the room flickered again in agreement.

Angel had sat quietly whilst Grizelle talked, but now she stretched over to put another log in the stove, before speaking. 'I told you to go within yourself before you made any decisions, Kirsty. What does that part of you say? Can you feel the truth, the authenticity in what we say? Dark times are coming to this town, and your gran wants to help from another place.'

She sighed sadly. 'You know what she was like, if she could have supported from this life she would have done so. There can't have been any other option for her. She was so connected, you know that, with nature, the earth, and the universe. There was no other way, Kirsty. And as hard as that might sound, you are involved in this, too.'

At her words, I felt something stir inside me. Sadness at my gran's passing definitely, but something else. I didn't know what, but perhaps a curiosity of some kind. Something in my genes, if you believe in things like that. It was as if she was suggesting that I had something to do, some role, a life purpose. Or perhaps that thought was way too fanciful for the situation. I knew I needed to find out more, and made up my mind I would go to the museum and library the next day to see if there was anything to find.

Grizelle left shortly after, and Angel and I relaxed on the sofas with some hot chocolate. I nibbled contentedly on the chocolate and nut cookies that were left.

'Is Grizelle still married, Angel?' I asked. 'She didn't really finish telling her story.'

'Sadly not. Gordon died about twenty years ago. He had a heart attack at his desk in Edinburgh. He died in the middle of a fraud investigation, and he left Grizelle penniless. There was such a scandal at the time. It was all over the newspapers, and Grizelle was horrified as you can imagine. I'm sure she'll tell you all about it some time, but she had to completely rebuild her life. I think it took her a long time to get over it, if anyone ever does with a sudden death. Sometimes it takes a long time for the shock to subside and for the person to find a way to live with it, with loss, I mean.

'Given that Grizelle and Gordon were never that happy, I think guilt probably came into that as well. I mean, she has such strong beliefs in the spirit world that it's not like she doesn't know Gordon is in a better place. I think it's more that she wished she had been kinder and found a better way to live while they were together. Guilt is such a destructive thing, isn't it?'

I wondered if she had realised what I felt about not speaking to my grandmother that final day, and shivered. I felt exhausted, so much had happened in the day and yet nothing at all, really.

'Angel. You know when you said you had *met* your Guardian Angel? Do you think I could do that sometime as well? It probably sounds mad, but I feel like it would take me closer to Granny, if you know what I mean. How would I do it?'

She gave me a gentle smile. 'Kirsty, you can do it any time you like. I do know what you mean about looking for that closeness. Would you like me to help? I run workshops at the café to help other people connect.'

'I don't know if you told me that, but I was hoping you could help me. Can we do it now?'

'Of course.' She put her hot chocolate mug down on the table, and stood up. 'Give me a few minutes to prepare. I'll go into the other room and take a moment to myself. It's always important to take these types of meditations seriously.'

She walked towards the door then stopped. 'Always use your own instinct, your gut response, to know if you have met the best teacher for you. No-one can choose someone for you. It has to be your choice, but I am so pleased you have asked me. Just let me take a few minutes to ensure my energies are clear and true. I'll dim the lights and put on some music to relax you, and when I come back in I'll take you through what we call a guided meditation. Basically, you go with my voice and see where it takes you in your mind. If you feel it's your imagination, then that's okay as well. This is about making you feel better, Does that sound okay to you?'

I nodded and made myself cosy on the big sofa, propped up on cushions in front of the candles and flickering stove. I pulled a large, pale lilac, fleecy blanket over me. It felt so comforting against my skin and I relaxed further into the sofa listening to the music. It had an eastern sound, with a woman's voice not really singing but more like holding notes. 'Toning' was what Angel had called it.

When she came back into the room, I smelt some incense and the music was turned down. I found that I couldn't open my eyes, it was as if something soft but powerful was holding me against the cushions. Not in a bad way or anything. I was so relaxed, I found I was on the edge of sleep.

Angel told me to take in a long slow breath, and then to release it slowly.

She spoke quietly, her tone soothing. 'Imagine you are sitting in the middle of a bubble of pearly pink light and as you breathe in it is filling your head, your throat, your neck and shoulders, your arms and hands, working its way down your body, into your heart, your torso, legs and feet. Feel your whole body fill with this palest pink light, and relax. Feel your body lighten. Feel any heaviness, any tension or stress soften and be replaced with the pink light. Feel it in your skin, your muscles, your blood. Think what it feels like to be filled with pink light.

'Have the word "peace" in your mind, see it in your mind's eye, hear it whispered in your ear, feel it surround you. Focus on what it would feel like to breathe in peace. Breathe in and breathe out slowly, relax, have only the word peace in your mind… let any other thoughts just drift away for now….'

Her voice had taken on a dreamy quality and I hovered on the edge of sleep, waking myself up as I almost dropped off, or so it seemed. Perhaps the whole experience was a dream. It felt like that.

'Kirsty, visualise a set of stone steps in front of you… they are taking you somewhere special… to a secret garden where only you can go… and your guests… people you want to meet. This evening you will meet your Guardian Angel. She is waiting for you at the top of the steps in your secret garden. Know that you are safe… you are surrounded with love and peace… Slowly climb the stairs into your secret garden. See all the beautiful flowers all around you, hear the sound of birdsong, smell the fragrance of your favourite flowers… this place is magical to you…

'At the top of the stairs is your Guardian Angel. If you want, she can come closer and let you sense her more. Feel her energies of love. She is here to help you with your life. She can share your worries, she wants to help. Nothing you can do, or have done, will stop her from loving you.'

At this point I could feel warm tears running slowly down my cheeks. Whether it was imagination or a dream, I did not know. But in my mind I had created a beautiful garden; multi-coloured flowers were all around me. I could hear birds singing and the distant drone of big fat bumble bees, and there were purple and pink butterflies darting in and out of the flower beds. Colours clashed crazily.

I was at the top of these old stone steps, and either side of me were plants and bushes in amazing colours of red, pink, blue, orange and yellow. I could see tiny little fairies in my mind, like fireflies lighting up my path. At that moment I sensed something coming towards me. It looked like a round rainbow of light. It didn't look like a person. Or at least, not like a human person.

It seemed unlikely even in my imagination that this could be an angel. But I asked: 'Are you my Guardian Angel?' I sensed it laugh… not in an unkind way or anything, more like in amusement. And that made me laugh, too. Like we were sharing a joke and really connecting.

The rainbow slowly opened up and revealed a being of light. I now knew what Angel had meant, because that was the only way to describe this vision. It stood about eight feet high, and was of the palest lemon and gold. I could see through it, but at the same time it seemed whole and solid. I was looking into a face as beautiful as any statue carved by an Italian Master, but with eyes which reflected back to me wonder and love. I realised that was the expression I was wearing as I looked at it. I didn't know if it was male or female, but that didn't seem to matter.

I could sense myself crying, my eyes were burning, and it opened its arms to me to walk into an embrace so light and yet so strong. I had the feeling that this Being could and would do anything for me. I only had to ask, and in that moment I realised that had always been my difficulty. For some reason, independence in my mind had meant separation, never asking for help. But this Being knew me, it knew all my foibles and had waited for me. I felt an overwhelming sense of love spread through my whole body. It felt good to be me, and I can't say I'd ever felt that way before. It was like the feeling you experience when you are in the first days of a new romantic love... but a million times better.

Very naturally, and in what felt like perfect timing, it released me and told me that it was always with me, urged me to tell all my worries to it, and said that it loved me unconditionally. With that, it seemed to retreat slightly, and I was aware of Angel's voice again, soothing me back to the sofa and out of my dream-like state.

'You know your angel is always with you,' she said. 'You can talk to your angel any time, or ask for her help. For now, thank her for joining you, retrace your steps back down the staircase in your garden, and I'll count back from ten... nine... eight... seven... six... start to move your body... feel your fingers and toes... five... four... stretch your body slowly... feel the sofa beneath you... three... two... one... take a moment... rub your palms together and hold them against your eyes. Do this three times, feeling the warmth from your palms on your eyes. Now take a deep breath and open your eyes.'

She didn't need to ask what had happened. My tears and distress must have been obvious, but now I felt relaxed, and really calm and centred. She suggested I drink a couple of glasses of water before bed, then left me sitting on the sofa, basking in the heat and light from the stove and from inside of me.

After a few minutes, I stood up, said good night, and went through to bed, hoping that I would sleep well after such a beautiful experience. Had it all been a dream? My imagination? It was so hard to tell.

It took me a while to fall asleep, part of me was still unsettled and worried by the experience at the hall. It had all seemed so alien to our little town, or was that the way life was nowadays everywhere? I kept re-running the meeting like a movie in my mind, still surprised at how quickly people had become angry with each other. No-one had listened to what was going on, and what about that group who had appeared? They looked like trouble to me, and I had a horrible feeling that worse was to come.

The church bells sounded out two in the morning before I finally slept. Again, I had strange dreams. This time I was in a cave and my gran was just out of reach. Every time I leaned out to touch her, a dark shadow came over me and I knew a horrible monster was waiting for me. This seemed to go on all night, waking and sleeping, waking and sleeping, until somewhere in my mind I knew I could ask for help. My angel! I asked her to come into my dreams to help me, and then exhaustion took over and I finally fell into a deep sleep.

17

I woke to the sound of Angel banging the external door on the way out of the flat. As had become my habit, I made a cup of tea and took it back to bed. Despite my rotten sleep, I felt strangely energised. It was as if I knew something was about to happen, but I wasn't worried. I took time to reply to texts from some friends in London who were worried they hadn't heard from me. I couldn't face talking to anyone yet, especially Derek, so I told them I'd be in touch as soon as I was organised.

I showered quickly, straightened my hair, and headed out to the town museum. Walking through the courtyard felt strange, and now that I knew what the pyramid was used for, I had a new respect for it. I didn't pop in to see Angel as the cafe looked busy and I didn't want to distract her. Instead, I walked down past *The Three Keys*. Grizelle's shop, *Serendipity*, was not yet open for business, and I was relieved as I felt I wanted to do this research alone and I knew she'd want to help.

At this time, most of the shops in the High Street were just opening up but there weren't many shoppers around. Outside the Memorial Hall I saw lots of litter where the protestors had dropped their leaflets and banners. One of the glass panels in the door was cracked, no doubt from last night's meeting, and a police car was parked outside.

I walked past the butcher's, the fishmonger's and the baker's shops, the bank and post office. Before crossing over to the Tolbooth – one of the oldest buildings in the town, and where the museum was housed – I shuddered as I saw a huge black rat squeeze itself through the drain and run down the gutter. It was horrible. Even though London was supposed to be filthy and my office building was located near to the Thames, I'd thankfully never seen a rat there. This was different. This was in the middle of a little Scottish market town, with countryside all around us. Field mice you might expect, but not a big black rat.

I shivered and walked over to the Tolbooth. I knew that black cats crossing your path were supposed to be lucky. But I wasn't too sure about rats.

A little bell tinkled on the door as I walked into the white two-storey building, and followed the signs through to the museum area. Huge windows overlooked the park which ran down to the river below, providing a stunning view, even in the winter.

The museum itself was small, with about six glass-topped cases stationed around the room. Inside were displays of pottery shards, coins, and clothing, with little white description cards explaining what each item was and where it had been found. There was also an exhibition area set out, with boards showing photographs of old buildings and a timeline of the town's history. I wandered from case to case as I'd done on previous visits. It all looked the same, and nothing really caught my attention.

At the information desk was the little bird-like lady who had held my arm at Granny's funeral. I couldn't remember her name. She looked even tinier than she had at the graveside. She smiled sweetly at me as I got closer, and I realised she had cataracts in her eyes so probably didn't recognise me.

'Hello, again,' I said. 'It's Kirsty… thank you for coming to Gran's funeral.'

'Oh my dear, it's so good of you to come and see me here. You must be lost without her. I know I am. She volunteered with me here at the museum, and I'm struggling without her. She could see so well, you know, and was always so fit and full of energy. I was just saying to myself that I so wish Kirsten was here, and then you walked in. It's as if she sent you!'

'Oh that's lovely, Mrs… Miss… Kilpatrick.' I managed to read her name badge. I hated getting someone's name wrong.

'It hasn't sunk in yet that she won't be back here with me. I think I'll have to give up my volunteering, I miss her so much…' Miss Kilpatrick pulled a little lacy-edged hand-kerchief from the sleeve of her green woollen cardigan and dabbed at her sightless eyes. For a moment I forgot my own grief as I tried to comfort this little, old, half-blind lady missing her old friend.

'I hadn't realised Gran spent so much time here,' I told her. 'Did she have a locker or anything? I'm trying to look through her things in case she left anything… for me.' I finished hesitantly. I didn't want to upset this lady any more than she was already.

'No, we don't have anything like that,' she said. 'We have a wee staff room through there,' she gestured towards the exhibition area, 'but all we keep are the tea things and some biscuits. Would you like to join me in a cup?'

I offered to make her a cup of tea but said I couldn't stay too long as I had so much to do. I had a feeling that she would have struggled to make a cup without burning herself, and it also gave me a few minutes on my own in the private area of the museum. While I waited for the kettle to boil I had a look around, but there was nothing to catch my attention, just some storage boxes of more coins and metal objects marked as found by the local archaeological society. The space was clean and tidy but uninspiring, and I couldn't feel my gran anywhere.

I left Miss Kilpatrick with a cup of tea and some chocolate digestives I'd found in the biscuit box, and decided to go into the library to see if there was anything for me there. Out in the grey drizzle once more, a sharp wind blew some rubbish along the street towards me. I winced as a protruding nail from a pallet box caught my calf, cutting through my trousers to rip my flesh. I had a horrible sensation of that black rat and some of its friends sniffing my blood in the air, and I shivered again at the thought.

Around the corner from the Tollbooth was Hope Street and the imposing sandstone pillars of the library. Like the Memorial Hall, it had been built when the town thrived. A glass and brass revolving door opened onto a wood-panelled entrance hall, and the smell of furniture polish and books tickled my nose. Sunlight from a large glass dome, high overhead, caught the dust particles and for a moment I thought it looked like the shape of a woman. As I blinked in astonishment, it disappeared.

I could see into the two large rooms either side of the main entrance, both were full of well stacked bookcases. In front of me, some steps led up to a glass door marked *Reading Room*. I had a feeling that's where Gran would have spent her time. I followed an arrow and a gold scripted sign saying *Local Interest* towards the back of the room, behind some high shelves.

Another sign pointed towards a large, dark, wooden door, marked *Private*. I turned the brass handle but it was locked, and there was no-one around to help. I walked back downstairs and found the librarians' desk in the first room to the left of the revolving door. There was a small typed sign apologising for staff shortages and explaining that staff were on other duties elsewhere in the library and would return in half an hour.

I sighed with frustration. I had pinned my hopes on finding something of my gran's at the library and I really didn't want to have to wait. At that moment I saw a little flutter of white wings at the very edge of my vision. It was like the moth from the graveyard. As I turned, I lost sight of it, and then it was at the edge of my vision again, like it was dancing out of sight but leading me back out into the entrance hall and towards the *Reading Room*. With another faint flutter, I found myself outside the locked room once more.

I had the strangest feeling in my stomach. The sign said *Private*, and the door was locked, yet something told me I was going inside. I hesitated for a moment, not sure what to do, when a little voice in my head said, 'You have my keys, my girl.'

18

Given that those keys had let me into the church, I shouldn't really have been surprised that my gran had a key for a locked, private room in the town library. I tried a few of the keys in the big brass lock before hearing a click, and I squeezed through the entrance, quickly closing the door behind me. With any luck no-one would know I was in here and I could take my time.

It was a long, narrow room, with high walls topped with ornate plasterwork. The floor was oak, and high wooden shelves were lined up along the walls, stuffed with books, documents, rolled-up maps and ribbon-tied parchments, some in open boxes and baskets. There was so much stuff I didn't know where to start.

The thick dust made me sneeze repeatedly. Some light came in from opaque windows on the ceiling, but it was dull outside and I couldn't see clearly. There was an array of plastic buckets and bowls along the top shelves and dotted around the floor to catch water leaking from the roof, so a smell of dampness added to the aroma of old paper. In the centre of the room were two large wooden tables, with an ancient-looking brass desk lamp on each, and two tatty, green, leather-seated wooden chairs.

The whole room was shabby, dank, and dismal, but for the first time I felt that this would have been a perfect place for

Gran to have left me a note. It would take weeks to go through everything, and I had no idea where to start looking. It had to be more obvious.

I had a quick scan through some of the shelves and saw lots of papers about the Town Council and lots of committee meetings; I knew it wouldn't be there. Over on the opposite wall, the books looked older somehow, leather-bound volumes, some with what looked like wooden covers. That looked more promising, and suddenly I realised I wouldn't find what I was looking for with my eyes.

I took a moment and tried to find that feeling I had experienced at the graveyard and again with Angel and Grizelle. I closed my eyes and breathed deeply. It was almost there, but it still eluded me. I was too anxious, too intent on finding something.

I sent up a silent prayer. 'Gran, please help me find this. Please show me.' And then, as an afterthought, I added, 'Make it obvious, please.'

As I finished saying this, my eye was drawn to halfway down one of the shelves labelled *Town History*. I noticed some books relating to the March Stones, volumes and volumes by date order of what looked like investigations and research. I wiped dust away from one of the books and couldn't believe it. The author was Kirsten Cairngeal Wallace. My grandmother!

I quickly looked through the rest of the books around it, but this was the only one with Gran's name on it. That had to be a sign, as Angel would have said! I carefully took the book from its place and laid it down on one of the tables, switching on the desk lamp as I did so.

The book was even more ancient-looking when I opened it up, and had been written on some kind of cloth. The first letter of each page was intricately painted like something out of an old bible, but the colours were vibrant despite its obvious age. It was written in an old-style script, each letter beautifully formed, and I realised that this was much older than something my grandmother could have done.

As I carefully turned over each page, I saw illustrations including what seemed to be copies of the stained glass windows at the church, and of our Stones. I could see the spiral pattern all around the edges of each page. It was difficult to read, as ageing had erased some of the letters, and dampness had caused some of the pages to stick together. This hadn't been written by my gran, but by an older relative a long time ago. I wondered if Gran had found it and been able to understand it better than I had. It certainly wasn't going to help me. I felt useless and stupid.

Reluctantly, I closed the book and turned to put it back on the shelf, but it slipped from my fingers and fell to the floor with a loud thud. Thick dust rose up and pages were dislodged across the floor. I dreaded anyone coming in and finding out what I'd done to what was obviously a valuable book. As quickly as I could, I put the loose leaves back into the cover and pushed it back into position.

As I did so, a little, red-covered book fell onto the floor. It must have been jammed into the back of the bookcase. I bent to pick it up and saw it was called *The Mysteries and Legends of The Old Toone*. A fresh white envelope poked out from within. I hardly breathed as I turned it round to see what was written on the other side. It was addressed to me. In Granny's handwriting.

19

There was a bang from somewhere deep in the building, and at the same time the lamp went out. I guessed that a fuse had blown, and even though I had never stolen a single thing in my entire life, I popped the book and the letter quickly into my pocket. I stuck my head out of the door and round the side of the shelves, but there was no-one around. The reading room was still empty, and now the overhead fluorescent lamps were out. I heard the sound of footsteps coming down the main staircase and the librarian telling people there was a power cut.

I joined a small queue to leave the building through the revolving door and the side doors, which had been opened by a worried-looking, grey-haired lady in the blue uniform issued by the local council to all its employees. I thanked her and smiled as I left. She had been one of the women who had left the meeting with us the night before, and she still looked upset. I didn't suppose this interruption to her routine would help.

The queue included some loud, excited kids who, from their uniforms, should have been at school, and some little toddlers and their harassed mothers. I walked quickly back up the High Street in the drizzle and light fog, not daring to look at my treasure until I was somewhere safe. Grizelle was standing outside her shop, as were some of the other shopkeepers. The electricity for the whole block was out, and her side of the street was in eerie darkness.

'Kirsty, looks like we've had a power cut,' she called to me. 'Did you notice if the bottom of the road was the same?'

The other worried shopkeepers were looking at me for an answer. It was not good to have to close for business in the middle of the day. As I started to explain that I'd been in the library and that it was also in darkness, there was a loud scream from the other side of the road. We all turned round to see a huge crowd spilling out of *The Cross Well* pub, which sat on the opposite corner from *The Three Keys*.

A fight had erupted and a couple of men were punching and kicking each other, while the on-lookers were pushing and punching, too. It was horrible to see and hear the noise of flesh thumping flesh, bone and muscle.

It was bizarre. One side of the street was concerned with sorting out electricity, the other was fighting and screaming. The faces of the people watching were contorted with sick pleasure, and more passers-by ran over to get a better view of the fight. I felt sick and turned away towards Grizelle. I didn't want to see it.

'Let's get some lunch,' she said. 'There's nothing for us here.'

We walked in silence up to Angel's shop, both shaken by what we'd witnessed.

'What do you really think is going on, Grizelle? That's two fights we've seen within a day… this isn't the town I knew.'

'Nor me,' she agreed. 'I get the feeling things will get worse unless we can do something to help'.

I told her about seeing the black rat and how it had given me the creeps, and she shuddered. 'That's not a good sign.'

I felt the letter and book in my pocket, but for some reason didn't want to talk about them out in the street. I waited until we were sitting down and Angel had joined us before I told them about my visit to the library, Gran's key opening the locked door, and finding the book and letter.

I could tell they were both really excited, and Angel leaned over to hug me.

'Hopefully you can get some answers and we can know more about Kirsten's plans,' she said.

'I knew she would get something to you.' Grizelle's eyes were shining with excitement. 'How clever you are working all that out.'

'Well,' I said, 'I don't think it was clever, it was more like following the signs. I don't think it could have been more obvious for me. Remember that little moth I told you about? It was there again, in the library… or at least, I think that's what it was.'

'Never mind how you got it, and don't feel bad about yourself,' Angel replied. 'I have a feeling it will help and make you feel better about your gran's passing. She loved you so much.'

At talk of my Gran, I felt a sadness fall over me again. The temporary lift from the excitement of finding the letter had faded, leaving me with melancholy again.

'I wonder…' began Grizelle. 'I wonder if something has already happened to the other Stones and that's why there has been such unrest in the town. We've been concentrating on the quarry, but what if some of the other Stones have been tampered with… just like the one in your garden.'

Her words sat between us all, connecting us in a feeling of dread and doom. I felt sick, and put down my last forkful of the hot apple pie and cream I'd been savouring.

'We'll have to go and see,' Angel said. 'There's no other way to be really sure. Is there?'

'Can we leave it until morning?' I asked. It was already lunchtime and we didn't have much daylight left. The fog wouldn't help.

'I don't think we can,' Angel replied.

'I really need to read Gran's letter before I do anything else,' I told them, hoping they'd understand how much it meant to me. 'I appreciate how important it is to check on the Stones, but I need to know what Gran wanted to tell me.'

'Of course, Kirsty, of course.' Angel got up from the table. 'You do that while we are getting things ready.'

Grizelle left to get her boots and waterproofs, and said she had spare pair for me and would be back within fifteen minutes. I left Angel speaking to her staff while I went round to the courtyard.

I had a sense to sit in the pyramid while I read the letter. I was desperate to hear from Gran, but at the same time I was really scared. What if her last words to me were of her disappointment? I still felt so guilty that I hadn't spoken to her properly. And so sad that I hadn't been with her when she died. Was that something I could ever live with?

Under the pyramid, I snuggled into the blankets and sat beside the crystals Angel had placed in the centre. I ripped open the envelope and gasped as I saw Gran's beautifully-formed, looped script covering the page. It seemed like another lifetime since I'd received one of those letters from home. The fact that this was the last ever hurt me so much more than I'd thought possible.

My hands were shaking as I unfolded it to read.

'My dear girl, first of all I have to let you know that I am incredibly proud of you, from the girl you were to the beautiful woman you have become. There is nothing you could ever do to change that. I love you always. Do not ever forget that you and I are connected forever in love. You are precious to me, my wonderful granddaughter and special friend. If you think of me, don't be sad. Imagine that I am in the next room. Not far away, and able to hear all that you say.

I ask now that you forgive me for leaving you without explanation of all that our family, you and I are here to do on this earth. Now that it's time to go I realise that I was a little afraid to tell you everything in case you were upset, and I lost you the way I lost your mother. I didn't want to put you through that. Please forgive an old lady who should have known better to trust that you would have understood. I am sorry.

So instead, I am telling you in this letter that you have to save the Stones. You cannot let them be moved in any way. They must stay where they are. Where they have been for thousands of years. It is our life.

Take the keys. They will guide you. Find the door and you will find me. I cannot say any more than that. Read the red book. It is not safe for me to write anything else. Words and thoughts are energy, and once they are out, others can sense them. I'm blowing you a kiss, my girl.

I love you more than life. Until we meet again,
Your loving Granny x x x'

It wasn't the explanation I'd hoped for, but the fact that she loved me and wasn't disappointed meant so much more than I could express. Relief and loss flooded through me. As if there was anything to forgive. I loved my Gran and she loved me. Until we met again, because I knew we would.

I cried for a few minutes, then a new resolve came over me. Gran wanted me to save the Stones, and I didn't care why. I would do all I could to save them. For her.

20

Traditionally, the walk around the March Stones – or 'Perambulation of the Marches', as was its official title – took place in early summer when it was usually dry, with long evenings lit until nearly midnight. No-one walked it in winter, but at least due to the cold weather, the ground would be frozen and not boggy. If we took torches we should be okay, and would be able to do it within a couple of hours.

Angel and I dressed in our warmest clothing, and she lent me a heavy waterproof jacket. Grizelle brought spare green wellies for me. She had a couple of little torches with her and a small day sack with some bottled water and chocolate, in case we got hungry. Grizelle suggested that we drive as close to the Stones as we could then walk the rest of the way. It would mean a meandering drive around the town, but given the weather and time of year it would be less difficult than walking from Stone to Stone across country around the town. The rivers were in full flow, so crossing over the forges or using the stepping stones, which were usually visible in summer, would be impossible.

Angel and I agreed and we set off in Grizelle's estate car, a much better option than Angel's old Beetle. On the way I told them about Gran's letter and how my feelings had been bitter sweet when I saw her writing on the envelope. I explained that I hadn't had time to look at the book, but felt there was more information that would help us. They were sympathetic and understanding.

We decided to start at Gran's house to make sure that our Stone was still in place. Arriving back at the house, it felt like a hundred years since my last visit.

We thoroughly inspected the ground around the Stone, but it looked strongly embedded and I couldn't believe it had been moved before. I asked Angel about that day and what she had been saying when she had wrestled the Stone into place.

'I was asking the angels and nature elementals – you know, like the fairies and elves – and all of the light and love to help me, she explained.

There was no point in asking if she really believed in them, as she so obviously did. I suppose at that point, despite my experiences, I still didn't fully understand.

'It worked, remember?' she added.

Angel and Grizelle stood on either side of the Stone with their hands lightly touching its surface for a few minutes before letting go. I didn't know what I was supposed to do, so leant against the tree nearby. It was as if I could feel the power of the tree through my coat, as if I was plugged into an electricity source, and at the same time a calmness overcame me. I had a sense that if I closed my eyes I would sleep forever and wouldn't want to leave the peace of the garden.

I realised that was how Gran had felt about this place. She must have been so connected. I wondered if the trees and plants knew she had gone. With that thought, I wondered if I was in danger of 'running away with the faeries', which was what Gran used to say about me when I was young. Funny how only a few days away from the rat race and all these fanciful notions were coming into my head.

Is that what work did for me? Stopped me using my imagination and feeling close to nature? Had I unplugged somehow and it was all here waiting for me when I was ready to see it?

At that moment, I heard Grizelle say, 'Each Stone is separate but connected. They tell me that all the Stones have felt movement beneath them. This Stone and the Thirteenth are in the most danger, as they are so close to the quarry. Kirsty, this is the first time the Stones have communicated with me, I think it's because you're here. Would you come over and touch the Stone?'

I couldn't. I just couldn't. I don't know where the fear came from, especially when I'd been feeling so relaxed by the tree, but her request terrified me.

'I don't want to, I don't think it would work for me anyhow…'

Angel came over and hugged me then took my arm, turning me away from the Stone. 'It's okay, Kirsty, it's all okay. We'll look at the other Stones as we're out, and finish at the quarry. You might change your mind… But there's no pressure.'

I sneaked a look at Grizelle, wondering if she was angry with me or disappointed, but she had walked ahead to the car. Within a few minutes we were on our way to the next Stone, which was set in the middle of a peaty bog three miles to the east. We had all walked these fields so many times over the years that we knew where to find the Stones without the need for maps or satellite navigation.

We parked in a layby and used the styles to cross a couple of fences to walk the mile or so to reach it. The cold wind rushed around us, as if hurrying us towards our destination. As we got closer, my heart was racing. *It was one thing to inspect them, but what would we do if they had been moved? What could we do?* I felt so exposed out here. This was so different from looking at the Stone in our garden. I suppose I hadn't really thought about what we were doing, but suddenly it struck me that this could be dangerous.

Thankfully, and I sent up a prayer of thanks in spite of myself, the Stone looked untouched. About four feet tall, it sat in the middle of its field, high up on the land, overlooking the town like a sentinel. It was covered with the same spiral symbols as our Stone, but without cups cut into the top of it.

Angel and Grizelle stood with their hands on the Stone for a few minutes, eyes closed and looking peaceful. It was as if they were listening or waiting for something. I didn't know what, and I didn't want to interrupt or interfere. But I was aware of the time passing and that we had another eleven stones still to check before I could get back to Gran's book.

It was as if they had heard me, and both opened their eyes and left the Stone at the same time. As she walked past me, Grizelle commented, 'We can't hurry this, you know, but all seems well.'

The third and fourth Stones were only a few hundred yards from each other, on two rocky outcrops about five miles outside town. They were close to one of the stone bridges which linked the town with the rest of the world. Without them, it would have been isolated on its island with three rivers flowing all around it.

We parked the car close to the bridge and walked back along the road, finding the muddy track which led up to the rocks. It was hard going this time, with the wind and sleet pushing against us, and we were all breathless by the time we reached the summit. I think Grizelle was the fittest of the three of us, and she seemed confident walking in the countryside. I couldn't keep my balance very well and landed on my backside a couple of times, blaming the wellies rather than my lack of coordination.

'That's what sitting at a desk five days a week and no exercise does for you,' I scolded myself.

Like at the earlier Stones, Angel and Grizelle laid their hands on top and listened. I found an old rock to sit on, and watched and waited for them to finish. As I did so, I again felt a connection. It was as though the rock was trying to tell me something; like the feeling I'd experienced from the crystal in Angel's home that first night.

I closed my eyes and breathed deeply, slowly letting my breath soften. A word was on the edge of my awareness, and I could sense it moving in and out before it receded. I thought about my gran but I couldn't visualise her face. Instead, it was something different – a man's voice, calling my name.

I stood up abruptly. That wasn't what I had expected, and Angel and Grizelle were standing in front of me, waiting for me this time.

'Anything?' I asked.

'The same,' they both said at once.

'And you?' Angel asked, and they both laughed a little.

I didn't want to say what had happened. *How could I explain that to them? To anyone?* So I fell in step behind them as we walked quickly back to the car. Out here high above the town, we could see a fog descending on the town, or perhaps it was lifting up from it. The light had started to fade into darkness and we moved a little faster.

We managed to find and inspect the next three Stones before night fell on us. The moon was hidden somewhere in the fog and clouds, and we had to leave our search.

Grizelle and Angel said the same things after touching each of the Stones. None of them had moved from position, but there was a sense of movement underground. Deep underground. I assumed it was the earth movement at the quarry. *Whatever else could it have been? If the Stones had been moved from below, what else could have been responsible?*

On the way back to the car, I walked with Grizelle. She linked arms with me and I had a sense that's what she would have done with my gran when they were children.

'Grizelle, can I ask you something, please?' I felt like I was five years old and expecting a scolding. She turned slightly towards me which I took as permission.

'Were you really disappointed with me earlier when I didn't want to touch the Stone? I'm really sorry if you were. I was a bit scared. I hope you understand and aren't angry.'

I winced, waiting for her condemnation. When none came, I chanced a glance in her direction. She was looking at me, really looking at me, and I realised how difficult I found it to look directly at people. I had got into a habit of looking all around with little bits of eye contact, rather than like this direct gaze from Grizelle. After a few minutes, I raised my eyes and looked back at her.

She said, 'That's better, Kirsty. When we can look at each other like this, we can sense so much more, can't we? There's nothing to be sorry about. There is no judgement involved. You are at liberty to do whatever you need to do. That's the truth. And it will make no difference to me. We are connected, all of us, but we have to make our own decisions. If something doesn't feel right to you, then that's your decision.'

'I thought you might be a little angry with me.'

'Why would I be? You have to do what's right for you, as do I. Perhaps you were disappointed in yourself and you were looking for me to validate that negative feeling in some way? I've found over the years that what we sense most in other people is what we have inside of us. I think the psychologists call it reflection or something like that. It amuses me that we never do that with fun and laughter, and happy emotions, though, do we? We usually do it with the negative stuff.'

She slowed down a little as we reached the car. 'Let me tell you what your gran taught me that a long time ago. When my husband died, I was so angry and I found I met anger everywhere. When he died, he was being investigated for a fraud. He had taken clients' money and spent it, and he was found out. It was a terrible time. For everyone. You see, he was a gambler. It was a secret shame of ours, and no-one knew. That's why he stole the money, to try and win back his losses, but he got caught. I was so angry with him and I didn't know how to express that.

'When he died I felt so guilty knowing that I hadn't supported him. As bad as it was that he was gambling, I was ashamed and angry at myself that he didn't dare tell me and that he must have been so lost and alone, and scared. For those weeks after he died, I was lost. I drank really heavily. To be honest, I'd been drinking too much for years.'

She paused and looked into my eyes. 'I know I can see in your face that you didn't know that. No-one did, or at least that's what I thought. I thought that I had hidden my drinking well. I was always careful to buy wine in different shops on different nights. I made up stories about having dinner parties and would stock up in out-of-town supermarkets so no-one would know. But, of course, Gordon knew, and your gran knew. She was always there, but to be honest that annoyed me, and I even stopped speaking to her for a while just before it all came out.

'So I lost my best friend because of my drinking, and then I lost Gordon and almost everything. A few weeks after he died, I knew I was going to lose the house and all my possessions to pay back all the debts. It was the right thing to do, but I was sitting feeling sorry for myself, drinking. I had the "me-me's".'

She lifted an eyebrow, smiling wryly at my confused expression. 'You know, poor wee me. Why me? Everything happens to me. You know what I mean? Well late that night, your gran turned up at my door with a van and four big lads. While I sat there, they worked their way around the house shifting out all my antiques and personal pieces. She told me to pack my suitcases, and we took all of my prized possessions, things that mattered to me like my mother's linen and good china, and lots of other stuff. I didn't know where we were going, but we all got into the van and she brought me to the back door of the shop.

'She had arranged with the landlord for me to have the shop and the flat above it for six months' rent-free. I moved in that night and opened the shop a couple of days later, then sold most of the furniture and pieces that we had taken from the house. I have no idea how we got away with it.

'The bank got the house and what was left. That house was full of stuff I'd bought but hadn't cared for so I really didn't mind it going. That was twenty years ago. Eventually, I let go of almost all the rest of the pieces, because I realised that they weren't important to me. I had no idea that I would have enjoyed my life so much, but your gran knew, and she was right.

'She was there for me when I thought most of the town were talking about me. It was only over time that I realised that they weren't being malicious and that they did care for me. They were all as shocked as I was, but they cared and showed that over the years by supporting my business.'

We'd reached the car, and she stopped before unlocking the passenger door. 'I stopped drinking then. Not immediately… There were lots of sad nights drinking my wine, feeling sorry for myself. But over time I felt better, and your gran was always around with her lotions and potions… and they all worked. She told me that I was a silly, self-obsessed woman, and to get over myself as we had work to do. And she was right!'

She gave me a brief hug before we all got back into her car and drove back to Angel's flat. When Grizelle dropped us off, we agreed to meet up the next day to cover the rest of the Stones in daylight. I had really wanted to see all the Stones were okay for my gran, and now we would have to start again in the morning.

I tried but couldn't shake the strange feeling I'd had when I'd heard that man's deep voice calling me. Still feeling unsettled, I left Angel to pop into her café to check on things, and I went up to the flat.

As I climbed onto the landing outside her front door, a wind whipped round and again I heard the man's voice calling out my name. Or perhaps it was the wind and my vivid imagination. I shivered and sensed the fog and cold night reaching into my bones, so quickly unlocked the door and put on all the lights. Then I closed the curtains and dropped the blinds against whatever was out there. The dark was now a place of worry for me.

I managed to light the stove, after a few attempts and lots of firelighters, and settled down to read the red-covered book I'd found in the library. It had a beautifully embossed leather cover, and as I turned the pages I could see that it was finely illustrated, like the much older book I'd dropped.

I turned to the front inside cover, but strangely there were no details of the publisher, edition, or dates. There was only a list of names and dates. Actually, to be accurate, it was the same name written over and over in different inks and different handwriting. My name, and that of my mother, and of my grandmother: Kirsten Cairngeal Wallace.

21

I t was a strange feeling, as if I had lived a hundred times before. I knew Kirsty was abbreviated for Kirsten, but seeing the name written in a long list hit me and I felt a connection, a whisper not just to my gran, but to her gran, and hers before her. I wondered if they had all been as close as we had been. *Did they understand that special relationship you could have with your mother's mother? Had any of them lost their parents young?*

For the first time, I wanted to know more about my family, my ancestors, and what they did to help the town. The realisation that it fell to me and that I was the last of the line struck me and I shivered; the lights in the room flickered as if to acknowledge the depth of my feeling.

I turned to the pages at the front of the book, but the tiny and ornate script was difficult to read. I couldn't make much of it out, but there were recipes and illustrations and I wondered if Gran had used these in her herbal preparations.

Drawings of the garden, with details of the plants and how to care for them, came next. All very useful, but not what I was looking for. Towards the back of the book I saw the illustration of what looked like the stained glass window from the church, the one with the dragon. The church must have copied this drawing. *Was that significant or not?*

I sat and stared at the picture, trying to work out what it was trying to tell me. Its message eluded me, so I turned over more pages and found an exact drawing of our Stone, then further on a map of all the Stones, with the town in the centre. *What was it trying to say?*

'Gran, or angels, I need your help,' I whispered. 'What am I missing?'

Why was this so hard? Why couldn't she have left me something easier to understand? With that thought, guilt and shame hit me. Gran had gone because she felt she had to, and here I was feeling sorry for myself. *Where would that get me?*

It was time for me to use whatever gifts I had inherited. I had to find a way to sort things out. There was information in this book and I had to find it.

I started again at the beginning, turning over each page slowly and carefully. There had to be something in it for me. I concentrated again on the map, and then the illustration of the dragon and maiden copied onto the stained glass window. I couldn't find anything significant on it, but that was hardly surprising when I didn't know what I was looking for.

I flicked over the last page and noticed that there was something tucked into the end cover. My heart was racing as I pulled out an ancient piece of parchment, like it had been torn from a much bigger page. I turned it over and grimaced when I saw it was a garish monster. A black, two-headed, horned beast, which almost leapt from the paper in fury. Red-eyes, its teeth were bared, and claws dripping blood. It was hideous, like something from a nightmare.

In the corner of the page was a five-sided star surrounded by a circle. The sign of protection from evil. It seemed appropriate to have it on this drawing. I folded the paper and popped it back inside the book. It was grotesque, but not what I was looking for.

I heard Angel come in and got up to offer to cook for a change, but she had brought a shepherd's pie which she quickly popped into the oven to warm. The aroma soon filled the flat and we ate in front of the stove, with large white candles flickering on the hearth, wax dripping onto the older collection.

I made us some tea and showed Angel the book. She flicked through it for a few moments before stopping at the map of the town and the Stones. Perhaps it was the angle she held it at, perhaps it was the food and relaxation, but for the first time I noticed what was sitting dead centre in the middle of the Stones. It was the church. And I knew then. Gran had said, 'Find the door.' She had already given me the key. I just had to find it.

My thoughts were interrupted by the sound of a knock on the door. I wasn't surprised to see Grizelle, and while Angel made more tea, I showed the older woman the book and explained what I'd worked out.

'Is that all too simple, do you think?' I asked nervously. 'That there is a doorway somewhere, and if I go through it I'll somehow see Gran again? Or will it help the Stones?' What had seemed so clear to me only a few minutes before was now as vague and opaque as the fog outside the windows.

'I'm sure it will all work out,' said Angel, bringing in the tray of tea. 'It's a sign, I'm sure of it.'

I felt like screaming at her, but managed to hold it back. Thankfully, Grizelle spoke before I could say react.

'I had an idea of how we can find out more about the Stones,' she said. 'I can't believe we didn't think of it earlier.'

Angel looked at her and laughed. 'Of course, we could dowse for it with a pendulum. What are we like? We know the Stones are telling us that it's the Thirteenth at the quarry that's in most danger. We don't need to go and see all the others, we can just use a pendulum to check if that's accurate. Now all we need is a map.' She looked pointedly at me and my book.

'What do you do?' I snapped in frustration. 'I don't know what you mean.'

'People have used dowsing and pendulums for years,' explained Grizelle. 'In many cultures, dowsing leads people to underground water, and farmers use pendulums to sex eggs so that they keep the females. All you need is something weighted to hang from a string, and you can ask yes and no questions. The pendulum swings to let you know the answer. Here, let me show you, it's easier if you see it in action.'

Angel opened one of the two long drawers in her coffee table and pulled out a selection of crystals of different shapes and sizes. All of them had a chain or string connected to one end, so that they swung down when she lifted them by the top of the chain.

'These are pendulums, and first you have to ask a question you know the answer to. For instance, is my name Angel?' She stopped and looked at the pendulum she had chosen from her collection – a drop of copper-coloured metal in the shape of an upside-down pyramid.

The pendulum moved on the chain, vibrating, then settling into a swing towards and away from Angel. She then asked, 'Is my name Kirsty?

This time the pendulum started swinging from right to left.

I had never seen anything like it, and my first thought was that she was making it move. She had to be.

'Try it,' she urged.

I picked up a lavender-coloured stone. It was about two inches long, with a clear crystal on top, and hanging from a silver chain. 'Erm… is my name Kirsty?' I asked, embarrassed. Immediately I could feel the pendulum tremble then it started to swing from left to right.

'Ask something else,' coaxed Angel.

'Is my name Grizelle?' The stone seemed to stop mid-swing then changed course and moved backwards and forwards.

'It's different for everyone,' said Grizelle. 'My "no" is when it spins round and round; my "yes" is when it goes from the right and left.'

I was still taken aback. 'So what do you use it for?'

'We can ask the pendulum to show us things, or tell us things, you know… to validate ideas we've had,' said Angel. 'I've used it to pinpoint where to put crystals or where to send healing. Tonight we can use it to check on the stones. And, if needed, we can use it to cleanse the energy.'

'How do you do that?'

'We ask for negative energies to be taken out. I use it in that way to cleanse rooms.'

Grizelle interrupted. 'I ask for negativity to be transmuted from furniture in the shop, and positive energies to be put in place. I guarantee when I do that the piece always sells quickly.'

'So how do you use the pendulum in that way?'

'You can sense it,' said Angel. 'The pendulum will spin anti-clockwise for negativity, then when it stops and I ask for positive energy it will spin clockwise. It's a simple tool but one which has probably been used since Stone Age times.'

'What will we do with it tonight?' I asked.

'We can use it over the map to ask if we need to go to any of the Stones. It will be interesting to see if it backs up what we learned today.'

Angel took my book and opened it at the map. She held her pendulum over the top and asked, 'Do we need to visit the eighth Stone?' The crystal swung from side to side, her signal for no.

She asked the same question for all the Stones until she reached the thirteenth Stone. This time the pendulum swung back and forward. Her signal for yes.

She asked, 'Is the thirteenth Stone safe?' The pendulum swung from side to side again. No.

Grizelle and I then did the same. We all had the same answers. The thirteenth Stone wasn't safe. We would need to visit it the next day, but I felt anxious. *What if we weren't on time? What if something terrible happened and it was all my fault?*

Grizelle left for home, and I wished Angel good night and went through to bed. My head was swimming after the day we'd had. I still wasn't sure if there was any significance in seeing from the map that the Stones surrounded the Church for protection, or whether that was a fanciful notion. Maybe I was just trying to make some sense out of everything that had happened.

It took me ages to fall asleep, and again I heard my name called. This time by a woman, but also a man. Whatever was going to happen seemed to be coming faster and faster towards me.

22

I woke early with the sound of the church bells sounding out six am. I couldn't get back to sleep so I made some tea and propped myself upon my pillows to read the red-covered book. It was hard to understand the script in the front of the book, but I found that towards the back it was easier, as if different people over the years had written and re-written key phrases.

Much of the writing related to what Gran had called potions and lotions, and I wondered what that kind of life would be like. Growing and using plants, enjoying a quiet way of life in a small community. Now that I had the house and some money, maybe I could return to live here, perhaps get some work from Angel or even at a local shop or pub. I'd pulled pints part time when I was at university, so I was sure I could do it again if required.

How easy would that life be? Would I be lonely and miss my London friends? Would I ever find love again? Of one thing I was certain. Derek would not be a part of this new me, wherever I ended up. Our relationship was over, finished. I wouldn't go back there.

With that thought in mind, my mobile phone buzzed with a text from my friend Jen. I called her quickly as I knew she was always up and on her way to the office by seven am.

She answered just as she was heading into the Underground station so we spoke quickly before she lost signal. I told her that I was thinking of staying, and waited to hear her scream at me. I felt sure that she'd think I was making a huge mistake.

To my amazement, she said, 'Go for it, Kirsty. If I had the chance, I would. Do you really want to be spending the rest of your life here? In a job that bores you? If I was you, I'd jump on the opportunity. This is a huge gift your gran has given you. When we were at university, you wanted to be a writer. Maybe this is your time to do that. Remember that movie we loved – Dead Poet's Society? Captain, my Captain?' By this time the signal was fading, but as if from another world I heard her whisper, '*Carpe diem*, Kirsty… seize the day!' And then she was gone.

I was shaken. I had expected… no, I had hoped that she would have laughed off my idea and told me to go back to London. Instead, she had told me what I would have told her. *Did I really need her approval to make such a major decision? Did I need anyone's approval? What had happened to the girl I was; the girl who laughed and loved, wrote and dreamed? When was the last time I had seized any day? Maybe it was time… what was the worst that could happen?*

I got up, showered and dressed, my head full of all the reasons not to move back home, then all the reasons not to go back to London. Home. Would it still be home without Gran?

I turned again to the little book. Somewhere within it was information that would help me understand what was happening to this town. My home. I read again those pages that I could make out, and flicked through it, looking for a clue, for something. Gran had told me in her letter to read the book. She'd told me to find the door and use the keys. *What other door in this town did the keys unlock? And how could I possibly find it?* I had found the letter in the book. They were connected. Connected but separate, just like the Stones.

I turned again to the map, which was drawn across two pages. That's when I noticed that one of the pages was thicker than the other. Some of the other pages at the front were stuck together with damp and old age, but there was something different about this.

I heard Angel leave for work as I went to the kitchen in search of a sharp knife and better lighting to look more closely at this thicker page. Carefully I prised one page from another, and at the back of the map found a short list written in tiny script. Someone had glued two pages together to hide this from prying eyes.

What had Gran said? Words were energy. She must have known about this list and hidden it in plain sight; it looked like the rest of the book.

It was a list of the Stones, nothing else. Nothing new. I let out the breath I was holding and it blew onto the book. My breath warmed the page and suddenly some words written in red ink began to materialise in front of me. As the paper cooled, the words disappeared again.

I couldn't believe it. *Was it a trick of the light? Or my over-worked imagination?* 'Angels, Gran, help me,' I whispered.

I walked over to the still warm kettle and held the page over the steam. A few words appeared as if by magic, across centuries, a warning. 'No blood on the Stones or…' The rest of the message was obliterated.

I felt the hairs on the back of my neck stand up. I felt sick. This was not a good sign. It couldn't be. What blood would be spilled on the Stones? Is that what had happened to the Romans? Did they sacrifice an animal on the Stones and it was their downfall? What did that mean for us? We wouldn't do a sacrifice, would we?

I knew I had to speak to Angel and Grizelle. At that moment my phone vibrated again. A text message from Angel: *Come downstairs as soon as you can. It's started. They're digging out the Stone at the quarry!*

I finished dressing, pulled on my hat and scarf, and the waterproof coat I'd worn the previous day, still with the little torch in the pocket. I didn't take my bag but put a ten pound note in my other pocket along with my gloves, then reached for Gran's keys and pushed them deep inside.

By the time I walked into the café, the place was busy. Everyone seemed animated and lots of copies of the local newspaper, *The Lanarkshire News,* were being passed round. Some members of the environmentalist group from the other night sat in the corner, finishing off their breakfast.

Angel waved me over to the empty table beside them, then left me the newspaper whilst she sorted out some tea and toast for us, and said Grizelle was on her way.

I noticed a woman in the group watching me as I read the headlines. Planning permission had been announced for the quarry extension, and there was a map of the new area. The Thirteenth Stone was to be removed and placed in the local Museum, according to the article, and excavation would come right up to the graveyard and all the way over to the wall at Gran's cottage. No, my cottage! What had been a tranquil place would have an open cast gravel quarry a few feet from the garden. This was outrageous! I'd had no idea it would come so close.

The woman from the group could see from the expression on my face that I was horrified. She leaned across to me. 'Don't worry, we're here to do all we can to make sure that doesn't go ahead. We'll chain ourselves to the equipment if we have to. We've done it before.'

I looked at her properly for the first time. She smiled and held out her hand to shake mine. 'I'm Sally.'

I introduced myself, but she said she already knew who I was. She had known Gran well, and expressed her condolences for my loss. I don't know what surprised me more, that she had known Gran, knew me, or that she was sympathetic, polite, and very well spoken. Not at all what I had expected.

She said she was originally from Cornwall but that her family were Scottish. She had been living at the peace camp at Faslane – the nuclear submarine site near to Glasgow – when she'd heard about the quarry expansion plans. She and some of the others had headed straight to the town, and wanted to do all they could to help.

'Your gran let us camp in the meadow at her cottage until the weather turned icy,' she explained.

I was shocked. I had been convinced that this group were aggressive and the cause of the fighting at the Memorial Hall, yet instead they seemed almost shy. One of the older men in the group, his hair closely shaven like Sally's, went up to the counter to settle their bill. The others joined in our conversation whilst they pulled on lots of layers of clothing. The day was bitterly cold and I wondered where they were staying.

'We've got a good deal at the caravan park coz it's winter,' one of the younger dreadlocked boys told me, almost as if he had read my mind. He had beautiful big brown eyes, with super-long lashes. 'We're getting by, doing some odd jobs round the toon. People have been really kind. Your gran let us take some of her veggies from the garden. Hope that's still okay with you.'

'Of course it is, not a problem,' I replied. 'Where are you going now? Are you going to the quarry?'

'Too right,' said an older woman, sitting at the edge of the group. Her long thick hair was white, and left to hang free like a young girl's. She wore a couple of fleece tops, scarves and shawls in every colour of the rainbow.

I felt so corporate in my black clothes and dark jacket. The thought ran through my head again: *when did I lose the colour in my life?*

Angel joined me as the group left, hugging them all in turn. I mean proper hugging. Not a quick air kiss like I usually did with friends, but holding each of them in turn. Nurturing them. Something else to compare with my life in London.

They had no sooner left than Grizelle arrived, and we all tucked into thick toasted bread and butter, with little pots of marmalade for them and raspberry jam for me.

'It's started,' Grizelle announced, as she sipped her tea. 'The whole town is in uproar. The *Lanarkshire News* published the story this morning. People are angry. The newspaper knew all about it two days ago and sat on it to get a reaction. Well, they got one alright. I think the editor will have to go. People are demanding his resignation. All the shops are shut; everyone is going to the quarry. There will be a bloodbath if they're not careful.'

I felt my own blood chill at her comment and explained the message I had found earlier in the morning.

'We have to go there now. This very minute,' Angel said. 'Let me get my coat and tell the girls where I'm going. We'll take the shortcut through the graveyard.'

Within a few minutes we were outside joining the hundreds of people on their way to the quarry. It was like the summer Lanimer's festivities, but rather than laughing and joking the people were angry. Heads down against the biting wind, we saw men and women of all ages, young children, teenagers in school uniform, babes in pushchairs, all rushing through the graveyard to save their Stone.

We walked as quickly as we could, taking one of the alternative stone-chipped paths as I didn't want to pass Granny's grave. Not yet; it was too soon.

The birds that usually perched along the top of the wall had flown off, disrupted by the throngs of townspeople cutting through to the far gate. From there was a well-worn path, although probably overgrown at this time of year, which ran the two miles or so to the edge of the quarry. I loved the view from the edge of town – the fields and paddocks, sheep and horses, the height and snow-topped majesty of Tinto Hill in the distance, the falls ahead of us, and the quarry hidden behind a range of old beech trees.

As we got to the gate, we heard people in front of us cry out in shock and despair before they disappeared from view. We soon realised why. Instead of the usual sheep-filled pastures acting as a buffer between the graveyard and the quarry, it was like looking onto First World War trenches. A couple of the older town residents stopped and stood to one side crying. One of the men had his head in his hands. I could hear people sobbing, 'Why? Why?'

The site had been transformed from lush greenery to twisted, exposed rock and gravel. Huge earth-moving equipment had ripped away fertile soil to expose the ragged edges of muck. The noise from the machinery was head-splitting, and we could feel the ground beneath our feet shake and tremble. Some of the little children put their hands over their ears.

The pathway from the cemetery came to an abrupt stop, and rather than meander downwards to the river below, it now had wide, mucky terraces cut into the ground, twenty feet or so wide, dropping down to the deepest point sixty or seventy feet below the graveyard gate.

People were still flooding through the gates behind us, each stopping to take in the full horror of their once beautiful vista reduced to rubble. They then stumbled and slipped their way through mud to stop on the terraces, sinking into muck and filth. There was a terrible stench in the air, as if a huge drain had been opened to spew out its poison. Some older residents from the local care home, which overlooked the scene, were out in their garden wearing pyjamas, slippers, and dressing gowns.

It was a bizarre sight. One half of the group wore hard hats, safety boots, and high visibility vests; on the other side of an invisible line stood ordinary people, toddlers in prams, schoolkids, the butcher and baker in their white coats, and all the other shop owners. Horrified, people stopped, stared, cried… and after a few minutes, raged and ranted.

Mobile phones came out, videoing the full extent of the damage to the land. As far as the eye could see towards the river and way in the distance towards the mountains, the land lay ripped open, exposed, vulnerable, and ugly.

In the distance we could hear sirens, and soon saw the blue flashing lights of a police car coming up the road from the quarry's main entrance point. It was as if everyone was waiting for them to arrive, frozen in horror at the tableau in front of them.

As we stood on a mucky terrace about twenty feet down from the graveyard, it was hard to believe that the earth-moving equipment could have made such short work of natural beauty.

I whispered to Angel and Grizelle, 'It looks like they've been working on this for longer than a few hours, doesn't it?'

We managed to slip and slither further down towards the front where we saw that one of the huge mechanical monsters had stopped at the March Stone; its steel jaws sat right at the Stone, scratching into the surface. The driver was still in his cab thirty feet above our heads. As we drew closer, we could see what had stopped its progress.

Sally and the older lady with the white hair had climbed onto the digger's heavy front blade. The rest of the protest group were lying down in a line, hands outstretched to each other like a multi-coloured paper chain of humanity. You had to admire their guts and stamina. It was freezing.

People on the terraces began cheering as news of their exploits reached them. Around us, loud whistles and shouts of encouragement broke out.

I looked at Angel and Grizelle. 'I've got a horrible feeling about this,' I warned.

After what seemed like an age, the police car eventually reached this new front line. I recognised the desk sergeant as he picked his way across the field towards the main digger and spoke to Sally and the older woman. Angel told me her name was Maggie.

By this time an official from the quarry had also arrived in another big truck. In hard hat and wearing a high visibility vest over his suit, shirt and tie, he looked important and more used to sitting in an office than being out on an exposed site. This company really meant business. It all looked very hostile as he spoke to the police then shouted at the group, and to anyone who would listen, that he had had enough and was moving the Stone whether the women were on it or not.

This only served to rile the police sergeant, who told him to get the site in order as he was surely breaking every health and safety regulation possible. Looking back towards the terraces and the gate, I could see more people pushing through, each one having their 'oh my god' moment as they took in the horror of the scene. It was like waking up to find a war had started in your garden.

Sleet was falling and a light dusting of snow lay on the ground, which was an excuse for some people to leave. Staff from the care home carefully guided their charges back inside, but after a few minutes we could see them standing at the upstairs windows not wanting to miss anything.

It seemed that the sergeant's words had had some effect on the quarry rep, as he moved to one side to talk into first a walkie-talkie, then a mobile phone. Assuming that the company was calling off the excavations, there was a cheer from the onlookers. But their hopes were short lived when more of the big machines began trundling towards us, and we realised that this was becoming a stand-off between the town and the quarry.

The biting wind, sleet and snow was affecting us all. My fingers were deep in my pockets but I was still freezing. I was sure Sally and Maggie sitting on the metal edge of the digger must have been icy cold, and the group lying on the ground would be in danger of hypothermia. We heard a helicopter circle overhead and saw that it was one of the Scottish news channels filming events.

Up on the hillside, someone began singing 'We shall not be moved', and soon the whole crowd was joining in. It was funny, but at the same time very moving. I had a feeling that Gran would have approved.

A shout went up and I turned to see some of the town councillors forcing themselves through the gate. They looked shocked to see how the machines had gouged out the beauty of the earth, even if they had agreed to it happening. As they made their way down the mud slide terraces, a couple of them slipped and fell, humiliated as the crowd jeered. It was unlikely many of them would be re-elected after this.

Six of the officials went forward, screaming at the police sergeant to get some sort of order restored and to get people away. It was obvious from the look on his face that he didn't have much time for council officials. He told them that he had called for reinforcements to protect the public from the quarry equipment, and that as far as he was concerned until he received official notification, the public had every right to be on public land. He added that he believed the quarry company was trespassing and could be charged with criminal damage.

The crowd roared its support, and I suddenly remembered that the last time I had seen the sergeant it was when he led his horse through the Lanimer's Day parade. He wouldn't be letting the Stone go without a fight. For the first time that day I felt my shoulders relax a bit.

We balanced precariously on the exposed rock and thick deep ruts cut into the mud, but with the high wind we were all in danger of falling over. I could feel my feet sucking and sticking, and most of the fifty or so people standing around the big truck were not dressed or shod for the conditions.

The sergeant approached Sally and Maggie and the group on the ground and suggested that they all relax, as it was likely to be a long day. He offered them blankets, clearly not caring whether he riled the quarry owners and the councillors.

None of the protesters accepted his kind offer, but the boys on the ground sat up, still in position, and then took it in turns to stand up and jump up and down for a few minutes. Someone squeezed through the crowd with some hot drinks for them, prompting another cheer from the terraces.

Apart from the cold, there was almost a carnival-like atmosphere… until we looked down and saw the huge ripped devastation across the fields. Hundreds of the townspeople now stood, waiting, on what was left of their hillside. Sleet and snow continued to flurry around us, and the sky darkened and lowered onto our shoulders.

'What are we going to do?' I asked Angel and Grizelle. 'This could go on all day, and look at the damage they've already done.'

They were both quiet, and I realised they were probably sending some healing to the situation. I stood slightly to one side and found my attention wandering towards one of the pools of water expanding at our feet. I could see a ripple dance upon it, like it was being shaken from below. It was filling with green, brown, and black dirty water. My mind played tricks on me. For one moment it looked like a huge dragon's eye staring out from under the pond. I shuddered involuntarily.

After another half hour, we were all freezing. My feet were like blocks of ice and my head was hurting. The crowd had thinned out slightly, so I offered to go and get drinks for us. Instead, Angel phoned the café and within ten minutes a couple of the staff arrived with trays of insulated cups filled with coffee and tea. She handed them out to the people standing closest to us. The hot drinks helped a lot, but as the day progressed, the cold wind and sleet showers thinned out the crowd further.

Another couple of police cars arrived, as did several lorries from the quarry, and a team of workers began to erect temporary fencing. But they could only go so far as there were still around fifty people still gathered around the Stones, including the police. The helicopter overhead flew off and then returned a couple of times, probably refuelling the engine as well as the reporters.

I was worried about Sally and Maggie sitting on cold metal, and the rest of the group sitting on the frozen ground. Although I knew they had a lot of layers of clothes on, they couldn't have been comfortable.

There was another shout from the crowd, and my solicitor Mr Douglas came sliding down what was left of the hillside. The same look of horror flickered across his face as he took in the carnage, before his professional demeanour returned. He slipped and slithered to a halt at the police sergeant, and between us and the councillors and quarry officials. He was tall, so we could see him clearly.

Mr Douglas cleared his throat and spoke loudly to ensure most of the crowd could hear him.

'In my hand,' he announced, with all the pomp and circumstance his three piece suit, silver watch chain, and mucky shoes permitted, 'is an interim interdict on behalf of the town. This document means that the quarry cannot move this Stone or take away a single piece of ground until a hearing at court next Monday morning.'

The crowd roared. Frozen limbs danced. The news was relayed by mobile phone to those further up the terraces and in the care home. Concerned faces turned into smiles and back slapping, and a couple of impromptu Highland dances and conga lines broke out. The sky was darkening all around us, and before long it would be dangerous for everyone on the site. The news had come in time and saved us all an overnight vigil.

The councillors shouted and argued amongst themselves and their officials; the man from the quarry had his head in his hands, his plans delayed until the court appearance.

A whisper, a breath, a shadow came upon me and I shivered. This wasn't over.

23

Flashes of lightning and the distant sound of thunder distracted me for a moment and I didn't notice some of the group trying to help Sally and Maggie down from the blades of the digger. The women were stiff from sitting on the cold ground all day, and had used up all their energy in the freezing conditions.

As they climbed down, the release of their weight shook the machine and the blades pushed ever so slightly against the Stone, toppling it over. As the machine moved, Maggie was too cold and stiff to get out of the way, and she fell back against the digger.

She yelped with pain and fell six feet onto the ground, her white hair quickly turning crimson as a huge gash opened up on her head, blood gushing out and dripping into the deep, dark hole where the Stone had rested.

I hadn't noticed that anyone from the doctor's surgery was in the crowd, but Dr McLeod and one of his nurses appeared from somewhere near the back and ran to Maggie, mopping up blood with a handkerchief. Clearly shaken, the digger driver climbed down quickly from his cab with a first aid kit and passed it to the medical staff, who were able to stem the flow.

We watched in horror as the soiled rags leached more and more blood into the pool of water and further into the ground. I swear I saw that dragon's eye blink for a moment.

Angel and Grizelle grabbed me and we climbed back as quickly as we could through the crowd, slipping and sliding as we joined the queue at the gate and into the graveyard. Linking arms, we supported each other in silence. In the semi-darkness, most of the crowd hadn't noticed Maggie's fall nor realised that the Stone had been toppled. Their mood was still jolly and relieved, trusting that the local court would not permit the quarry expansion.

I heard lots of people saying 'over my dead body will that happen' as they headed confidently home. And although it was an everyday phrase, I shuddered with fear.

'Kirsty, it will all be okay.' Angel, as always the nurturer, sensed my fear. 'Let's get inside and warm, then we can think about what to do.

But I just knew that something terrible was about to happen. Looking at their pale faces in the gloom, I knew that she and Grizelle shared that same thought.

I heard the church bells ring out five o'clock, and it was dark as we walked through the burial ground. We could hear other people walking around us as we slipped and scrambled to walk on the icy pathways. My stomach churned. Something terrible was going to happen to the town.

I turned to Grizelle and Angel. 'That's the bells for five o'clock, and it's already black out here. Look, we can't see a star in the sky. What can we do?'

Grizelle and Angel both turned towards me like synchronised spirits in a dance of the living.

'Kirsty,' said Angel, clearly perplexed. 'What did you say about the bells? Did you mean the church bells?'

'Of course.' I shook my head in frustration. 'I hadn't realised that they'd been fixed until I got back. I've hardly needed to look at my watch since I came here.'

Grizelle's placed her hand on my arm. 'Kirsty, the church bells weren't part of the restoration; they're still in storage. The church hasn't had bells for over forty years.'

'But I've heard them. All the time.' I looked from one to another. 'What do you think this means? How can I hear something that isn't there? Like phantom bells?'

'Or a sign from Kirsten only for your ears. Just for you.'

My feet were still frozen, my hands and cheeks icy, but inside me something burned. I could feel my gran close by my side, my mum, dad, generations and generations of Cairn-geals firmly behind me. They were right.

'We have to go to the church tower,' I urged. 'It must be the door we need. Come on, quickly. '

24

We made our way quickly out of the grave-yard's main gate, three women with a common mission. I had no idea how much time we had or what would happen, but the book's warning had been clear: no bloodshed on the Stone. And by accident, fluke, or some much older design, blood had been spilled and the Stone had moved.

The main road was almost empty of traffic but full of people heading back to their warm and well-lit homes. An ambulance passed, no doubt carrying Maggie for a check-up at hospital. We didn't see the rest of the campaigners, but I was sure they would be given a warm welcome everywhere in the town once word of their heroics got round.

When Angel, Grizelle and I turned into the church grounds, the lights were all out. It might have been another power cut, but the street lights were still on so I had a sense that something darker was responsible. The normally floodlit cross was in darkness, and no moon or star was visible in the velvet black night sky. Grizelle led the way to the main door and then turned right towards a small wooden door, hardly visible in the shadows.

'This takes us into the tower,' she explained. 'It's always locked for safety reasons, and I'm sure they blocked up the inside door from the church into the tower years ago. This is the only way in, but I'm not sure what's there. The bells were taken down and put into storage years ago. I'm hoping the steps are okay.'

We couldn't see much, especially with the old wooden door being in shadow from the church and the square stone tower over one hundred feet above our heads. I pulled Gran's keys from my pocket and put one into the lock. It didn't turn. Neither did the next, nor the next. None of the keys fitted.

I tried them all again convinced that I'd missed one. We didn't have a key for this lock. *Could I have lost a key in the last few days?* I didn't think so. *Could Gran have hidden one away somewhere else? Why wouldn't it open?* It had to be the Tower. I was the only one hearing bells. It had to be a sign.

'Angel, Grizelle, is there any other way into the tower? Another doorway? I'm sure there is a connection with the bells. You both feel that too, don't you?'

They nodded in agreement, shadows playing on their faces, contorting their features but I could sense their growing excitement.

'It has to be here. If it's to do with the bells, then where else can this lead but here to the bell tower?' I was muttering to myself as much as to them. 'There must be another way in, or is it another place, where the bells are? Grizelle where are the bells stored? Would Gran have known?'

I was beginning to panic. I didn't know how much time we had and I didn't know what would happen. I had a horrible feeling of dread, but at the same time I wanted to get this sorted, do whatever I had to do. I was doing it for Gran, and all my family across the ages.

'I think the renovation company have the bells, but I don't know where that is. It's not in the town, I know that for definite,' Grizelle replied. 'There has to be another doorway.'

'Let's go up to the flat and have another look at the book,' Angel soothed, putting her arm round me to stem my panic. 'There could be something else in it.'

But I knew there was nothing else in the book to help. I had to figure it out.

I stepped back from the two of them and the shadow of the church then walked to the end of the tower, feeling the brickwork. I was working on senses, on instinct. Something had my attention, and this time I wanted to follow it through to wherever it led me. No matter what or where.

'Angel,' I asked. 'What's on the other side of this wall?'

'It's the lane between my building and the church wall.'

Although I couldn't see their faces, I could feel they were turned towards me, attentive, in tune.

'So the side wall of the church tower is against your wall?' I could feel excitement building. 'Do you know if there is a doorway in it? I've walked up and down that passageway a dozen times since staying at your flat, but I've never noticed anything. Have you?'

We walked back towards the street and welcome overhead lighting, and I saw her blond curls shake sadly.

'Sorry, Kirsty, there isn't a doorway on that side of the wall. It's a great idea but I would have noticed. There isn't a door, only stone walls.'

There was something tugging at the edges of my mind; a feeling, a word of inspiration trying to get through.

'Let's go and look anyway. It's a feeling I have, and you did say to go with my feelings. I know it doesn't make any sense but I feel we are really close to something. Will you come with me and look?'

Deep down, I knew they would come. These two women had been at my side for the last week, supporting and helping me.

The light from the street lamps cast a yellow glow a few feet into the alley between the café and the church wall. I walked into the dark space first, followed by Angel then Grizelle. Immediately I had a sense that the energy had changed. It was like walking into an invisible force field of some kind.

I felt Gran draw close, whispering in my ear, and I stopped three-quarters of the way down the path, directly on the other side of the wall from the tower. We could sense its vastness above us. It was dark –, no stars, no moon, and still the distant rumblings of thunder. Sleeting heavily now, I could faintly see a fog coming in and swirling around our knees.

I pulled out the mini torch I still had in my pocket, and we all held our breaths as I shone it up and around the wall.

Angel was right. No doorframe or door was visible. We all sighed in frustration. But I knew I was close. *What was I missing? What else was there to see, to know?*

'Come on,' Angel whispered. 'Come upstairs and we'll meditate, that might bring in some help for us. It'll be fine, Kirsty. We'll sort this. Or we could try our pendulum. I have faith in you, Kirsty.'

Grizelle and Angel turned and began to walk away, but I couldn't. Something was keeping me rooted to the spot. I shone the torch again all around the stone wall, convinced I was missing something. I took off my gloves and rubbed my cold fingers across the rough stone surface, feeling it scratch away the skin at my fingertips. Nothing.

I briefly closed my eyes and sent up a message yet again to Gran and my angel. *What am I missing? I know it's here. I know it. What am I missing? What am I looking for? Help me, please.*

I took the keys out of my pocket and looked at them in the torchlight, then looked again at the wall. *I need a keyhole.*

'I've been looking for a doorway,' I called to the others, 'but actually all I need is a keyhole!'

I dropped down to my knees, darting the torch back and forward over the wall. Feeling every mark, every edge, the unevenness of the wall with my fingertips.

'What's this?' About four feet up from the ground was a small hole. An inch or so long and wide. Almost invisible in the ancient stonework. 'I've found something!'

Angel and Grizelle returned to my side as I shakily stuck a key into the hole. It was big enough to take the key, but I didn't feel any connection or the sound of steel or anything to tell me that it was a lock. I tried the next key; same again. Tears of frustration came to my eyes but I took a deep breath and tried the next key.

I heard it connect; I had found a lock. A hidden lock. Gran had told me to find the door and use her keys. I had done it! I turned the key back and forward a couple of times. It was stiff, and I sensed the pressure as centuries-old mechanisms creaked. Then we heard a faint click as the lock released. I pulled the key out and put the bunch back into my pocket.

I bent down on my knees, feeling the cold dampness through my jeans, and pushed against the wall with my shoulder. Nothing shifted. Nothing moved. I took another deep breath and pushed really hard with all my weight against the wall. Angel shouted a warning as a hidden doorway opened up, but I was off balance and fell hard and fast into the blackness beyond. The door shut abruptly behind me, leaving me alone inside and Angel and Grizelle standing in the dark alleyway without anyway of unlocking the door as I had the keys.

25

I fell only a few feet, but there was total blackness and I screamed in terror before hitting wet soil face-first. The wind was knocked from my lungs, and it took me a few minutes before I could sit up. I panicked as I tried to find my bearings in the dark. I knew the doorway must be somewhere above my head, but not exactly where.

Left, right; I had no internal compass. My eyes hadn't adjusted to the blackness and I couldn't see a thing. I rubbed my freezing cold hands over my face. My forehead was grazed and I could feel wetness which I assumed was blood on my scratched fingertips, but I was okay. No bones were broken and nothing was damaged, just sore and bruised.

I was cut off from Grizelle and Angel, and I guessed they would go and get help once they'd recovered from the shock of seeing me disappear through a hole in the wall. The door must have sprung shut behind me, and I had the key so if I could keep calm I would be rescued eventually. The police would still be at the quarry, so realistically it would be a while before they could get back into town. The main thing, I told myself, was that I was unhurt. Scared maybe, and uncomfortable in the cold and dark, but overall I was fine.

After a few minutes the shock of the fall and my situation started to fade. I couldn't hear a thing from above through the thick stone walls. I couldn't see a thing, not even my hand in front of my face. I decided to try and feel around me to see how big the space was.

I assumed I must be in the bottom of the church tower and attempted to stand up, only to hit my head on a roof of some kind. I winced with the pain. The opening I had fallen in must have been at the top of this space. I carefully felt around and above me using my hands, then moved along on my knees to try and find the edges of the room. I hit the wall about two feet from where I was sitting ahead of me, behind me, and to my left. On my right hand side, I stretched out into nothingness. I wasn't sure whether I was in the tower or in a space between the walls.

It was cold, dark, and silent. I felt it might be safer to stay kneeling down to avoid bumping my head again, so I slowly edged forward, using my hands in front of me on the floor to feel for the other wall. Instead, I found myself moving further and further along the floor, which felt dank and dirty. I wasn't sure whether it was earth or dirt-covered stone. There was no way to tell in the darkness.

I was trying to focus on my breathing. I had a sense I was on my own, there was nothing around me. As I settled into the silence, it felt peaceful. I sensed there was nothing to be scared from; rescue from above might take some time, but I'd be fine. *I'd do some safe exploring*, I told myself, and then I could turn around and feel my way back to where I'd started. *I didn't have to worry. Rescue would come eventually.*

I was trying to modulate my breathing and keep calm, ignoring my aching knees and sore head, when I saw a faint flickering light a little bit ahead of me. Instinctively, I moved towards it. It would be the torch I'd had in my hand when I had been examining the wall. It must have fallen away from me, and was almost out of power.

I crawled slowly towards the light. But rather than get closer, it remained at a distance from me. Then my hands hit the edge of the floor. I sat back, confused, not sure what was happening. The light seemed to have dropped down a bit further ahead of me, and I realised there must a staircase. The light was coming from down below.

I groped around and felt some steps, then turned around so that I could go down feet first, one stair at a time. The light had stopped moving now. It was as if it was waiting for me to catch up.

Using my feet, and still feeling gingerly all around me, I found that the steps were about a foot wide, and six inches or so high. I could feel stone at either side, and from the dank, damp smell it was as if they had been cut into rock. They didn't feel smooth, but were jagged and rough. I was still surrounded by darkness, but the little light that kept appearing from below showed me some parts of this narrow staircase appearing to be cut from solid rock. It was as if the earth itself was opening up to me. Gran had said in her letter, "find the door and find me". I had a crazy feeling that this would lead me to her.

Step by step I followed the little light which was twinkling and dancing ahead like a firefly. Each time I thought I'd lost it and couldn't physically go on any more, it appeared again, teasing me with its promise of light in the darkness. Thoughts of seeing my Gran as crazy as that seemed kept me going.

It was getting colder and wetter. I felt drips on my coat from little springs and fissures and my trousers were soaked, but still I moved slowly, carefully, further and further down the stairs trying to catch the light. After what must have been ten or fifteen minutes and I was beginning to tire, my feet hit what at first I thought was a wider step. The light had disappeared, and I stopped in the darkness, stretching my fingers out to feel what was next.

The ground felt level, so I turned back around and crouched down, then moved forward in the darkness, crawling on hands and knees into what seemed like a tunnel. I stretched out my hands. I could feel the walls on either side me and the ceiling above me, perhaps four feet or so, not high enough for me to stand up.

Way in the distance I saw the light flicker and I crawled along the tunnel towards it, hoping that there was some other way out and that I wouldn't have to find my way back again.

I'm not usually claustrophobic, but in the darkness, banging into rock with my elbows and knees, scratching my head on the low ceiling, I could feel little flutters of panic rising in me. This was so outside of my usual comfort zone, but focusing on my gran kept me going. I knew she'd laugh if she could see me; she knew I hated exercise and this was like an assault course in a freaky house of horrors in blackness.

The light had disappeared and I found myself in complete darkness again, edging along in silence, with only the sound of my breath and the scuffling of my coat against the wall sides.

Suddenly my head connected painfully with something solid, and I stretched out my hands in the darkness to feel a rock wall. I had reached the end of the tunnel. There was no way out. In the black silence, I screamed tears of frustrations, fear and panic, and the horrible realisation that I'd have to back up all along the tunnel. There wasn't space to turn around.

That was when I cried. Rocking myself back and forward in an attempt to comfort my sadness. The combination of loneliness, frustration, confusion, and a tinge of self-pity overwhelmed me, and I sobbed for help in the emptiness of the earth. I knew it was futile but I didn't know what else to do. I'd followed the clues; I really cared; I wanted to help. But I was lost, lonely, and scared. I was here for Gran but she wasn't here. *What a fool!* I should have waited in the upper chamber to be rescued. Now I'd need to find my way back.

At that moment in the blackness, I was aware of a sound a little bit behind me on my left hand side. I wasn't sure what I'd heard, like something hitting metal. I frowned and waited, holding my breath as I listened. There it was again. Faintly to my left, and slightly behind me. Like metal striking stone. Maybe there was another way back to the surface

I quickly crawled in reverse and managed to back up a bit in the tunnel towards the noise. I caught sight of the light again, as if it was waiting. I'd missed a turning! The little light stopped, and I moved towards it again. I still wasn't sure what had made the noise, but I whispered a prayer of thanks and hurried along. I was still in darkness, with the little light dancing ahead and the odd sounds of metal hitting stone.

I must have gone in about twenty or so steps when the light ahead of me stopped. It started to expand, and now that it was closer I could see it was more of a blue than I had noticed. I sat back on my feet and watched it rise slowly higher and higher, and realised it was showing me that the tunnel had opened up into a huge chamber. As the light increased in size and brightness, it flew around, rising high and wide, to show me that I was now in a huge cave.

I could hear water running off into the distance somewhere, while the cave itself looked like it had been cut out of crystal. It resembled Angel's piece of pink quartz and some of my gran's stones. The light dazzled off the walls of the crystal cave and flew down to the bottom, where I could see a large, tranquil, turquoise lake.

I stayed where I was, looking all around me, taking in the whole space as it was lit up by the dancing light, as if putting on a show for an exclusive audience of one. The cave was beautiful, like something out of a dream.

Suddenly, just as I appreciated the beauty of my surroundings, the light started to slow, contract, then drop down towards me. As if it knew what I was thinking, and sensed I was calm and open.

The light slowly came closer to me, and I could see it was a deeper blue in its centre. It was a ball; a sphere the size of a football. Deepest blue in its centre and then becoming more white and brighter at its edges.

It stopped a few inches from my head, its centre level with my eyes. I flinched a bit as it came closer and I felt it move in towards me, touching my forehead. I could hardly breathe as I felt its warmth, its energetic tingle, and my head filled with images of Gran. Of her and me together, like a photo montage of our whole life together. I heard her voice. I felt her strong arms around me.

This was her. She was some sort of ball of light, of energy. And through my tears, I knew why she would want to be in this state, why she would want to return to this state, because as light she was powerful and connected. She told me or showed me – I'm not sure how I understood – that this was what death was like. A return to love for everything.

I opened my eyes and looked straight into the centre of this blue ball of light and I just knew it was her. It was like the sensation I'd experienced when I'd met my Guardian Angel. I felt love and strength, and that we were still connected. Nothing was going to separate me from her. Death was not the end. And that thought came with waves and waves of emotion. I didn't have to say sorry for anything. She knew everything… because she just did.

The light ball started to move away from me, but that felt okay; I knew it would not go far. It moved off to light a path for me through the cave and off to the left hand side, where its illumination showed a huge thirty or forty feet high piece of crystal. I couldn't have stood up at that point; I didn't trust my legs to hold me. So I crawled through dirt and muck along the side of the lake, towards and then slightly behind the crystal rock.

The light ball dropped down towards the floor and there in front of me I saw a huge metal padlock firmly holding three large chains. I sat back on my heels for a moment, not completely understanding what I could do to help. As my mind considered all possibilities, the light ball suddenly swooped down towards my pocket and then back to the padlock.

It was telling me to use the keys to unlock it! At that moment I saw one of the chains tighten, and I heard a roar and a flash of flame somewhere deep in the heart of the cavern. I screamed, and there were more roars, animal screams, high-pitched and accompanied by flashes of fire, high up. I smelled burning, like bonfire and heard what sounded like wings flapping in flight.

When we'd been at the quarry site, I'd thought I'd seen a dragon's eye in the water. *Had I been right? Were there trapped dragons under the earth, and the light wanted me to set them free?* Surely not. It didn't make sense. Dragons didn't exist. *How could they?* And if in some bizarre way they were here, they had to be chained up for a reason, to keep us safe. I wasn't going to be the one to release them. I finally got to my feet and tried to run back towards the tunnel but, apart from the occasional burst of flame above my head, the cave was in darkness again.

I stopped and turned around. The blue ball of light was behind me, and slowly it transformed into the shape of a woman. Faint and opaque, and with the same blue centre and white outline. It was like looking again into the face of my grandmother, and I wept, stretching out my arms to try and hold her. In my mind I felt her arms around me, and I took strength from that. I heard her whisper, 'Do it, Kirsty. Free the dragons, we need their help.'

As I wiped my eyes, she returned to her sphere state and flew across to the padlock again, lighting my way. I fell down on the floor and pulled the bunch of keys from my pocket. I hesitated, my whole body trembled with fear. *How could this really be happening?* The ground started to shake, and I heard a roar and the sound of something large moving towards me. From behind the crystal rock I was aware of a movement, a presence of some sort rising high above me. I could hardly look and covered my face with my shaking hands. More scared than I'd ever been in my life. I was sure I would die, trapped somewhere underground, my mind unhinged. Nothing happened. I felt a warm breath on my face. I chanced a glance up and found myself looking into the lizard like eyes of a dragon. A real dragon. Its huge head crisscrossed with scars. Even though we were in semi darkness I could see it clearly. We were so close. I dared not take a breath. I tried to back up a little. Slowly, calmly, gently, hoping it wouldn't notice. Because after all, how long had it been chained up, and *how hungry was it?* It saw me. Or to be more precise it watched me. As if I was the strange creature. It stood twenty feet above me, and from behind it I heard the shuffle of other creatures, pulling against their chains. Panic swallowed me, I scrabbled to get away, sobs in my throat, fear taking over my whole body.

At that moment, the blue sphere appeared again, rising between us. Lighting us both up, and with the light, the dragon fell back. Almost as mesmerised as I had been with the light. It looked at me again, and in that moment I realised it wouldn't hurt me. I knew I had nothing to fear. I don't know how but I just knew it. The dragon was there to help. I had to trust that this was the way it had to be. I threw myself down at the padlock, and with shaking hands I eventually found the right key and heard the click as it unlocked. Immediately I heard a roar and the beat of wings and shadows on the wall as three dragons flew off high into the cavern. Spitting fire was all I saw, and the shadows of their wings. I didn't know where they had gone but I heard them squeal and roar far ahead of where I sat.

My body was shaking and I remained sitting on the floor. The light ball flew off again, then returned, and flew off again. I knew it wanted me to follow, but I was terrified. I'd trusted that releasing the padlock was the right thing to do, but I wasn't sure how. I could hear the roar of flame-throwing, smell burning hair, and animal shrieks reverberated throughout the cavern.

Instinctively, I knew I had to follow the light towards the dragons, but first I needed to take a moment and gather my thoughts. The light ball returned to me, and waited as if it understood my fears, then it came close again towards my head. The chamber seemed to lighten and brighten, urging me to look behind where I sat.

I turned round expecting to see more darkness, but my eyes were filled with light. I could see hundreds and hundreds of figures, like people but full of light, and as I looked at those closest to me, my head was filled with visions of my mum, and my grandparents. I realised or they told me, I don't know which, that these were my ancestors. Hundreds if not thousands of light beings at my shoulders, stretching off into the vastness of the cave.

I had a sense that they were telling me that they were always with me. That I was never on my own. That they were with me to bring strength, love, anything I wanted or needed. I remember thinking that if everyone knew that, people would have no need to be afraid of anything. If we all knew we had this resource, why would we worry about living or dying?

I was suddenly aware of another being standing off to my left hand side. I sensed this was a man, and beside him were Angel and Grizelle. Or at least, it felt like them. They each had hundreds and thousands of light beings with them as well. I had an idea that we were all an army of light, and that whatever we would fight would not stand a chance. I immediately felt filled with power and strength.

This all happened simultaneously, but without words, as though we could all communicate into each other's minds. Time meant nothing in this expansion. At that moment, all the beings rushed forward, gathering me up with them, and we soared and flew onwards in the trail of the dragons. With this light, I could see all around me as we powered through rock and space. I knew that we were all the same, connected, everything that had ever been or would be. I was rock; I was air; I was the dark and the light. There was no separation, and my heart filled my chest with happiness. I was unaware of my physical body, and the earlier discomforts of pain, and cold, and wet had disappeared in this incredible feeling of togetherness, of love.

Within moments we were in another cave, a much bigger cavern than the last. Our army of light waited somewhere close to the roof of this incredible place. A smell so disgusting hit me and I swallowed down the bile. It had a metallic odour, like blood mixed with ammonia, and something else I could not place. Far beneath me I could hear the screeches and screams of the dragons, and see the occasional fire and flame from their mouths, and the shadows of their wings as they turned one way and another in an attack on another creature I could not see. The acrid smell of burning flesh and hair threatened to make me vomit.

The blue ball of light dropped gently downwards, and as she did she expanded again, the way I'd seen her do before. This time she became bigger and bigger, filling the whole cavern with bright blue and white light.

It was only then that I noticed that the cavern walls were moving, undulating in the light. This was what she wanted to show me. I felt the light of my ancestors draw around me like a protective shield from the horrors of this chamber. With the screaming from the dragons below, dark, darting shadows, and the disgusting stench, I knew this was a place of pain. And with a start I realised the smell was death. This was what Granny had called Ifrinn – the dark earth. Hell.

26

As the light ball expanded, more and more of the chamber showed up in greater detail. I could see that it wasn't actually the black walls which were moving back and forward; we had nothing to fear from those. What I saw in the light were individual corpses hanging from the walls and roof. Each corpse – with tattered skin and clothing, some still with eyes, and soft tissue, and tufts of hair – was just about recognisable as a human being.

As far as my eyes could see in the slowly lightening chamber, thousands and thousands of souls were kept in place, pinned by a thick black cord of what looked like some sort of liquid, skewering them through their hearts. Their screams of mortal agony brought tears to my eyes. As I watched, I saw each haunted corpse of humanity have its life sucked out with a pulse through the black cord, leaving them to hang as blackened, burned, lifeless skeletons, frozen in time and space for eternity, or so it seemed. Then, with another pulse through the black cord, they transformed again into the haunted corpses. Screams of agony filled the chamber, adding to the noise of the dragons fighting something below us. *What could these people have done that was so bad that they had no chance of rest even in death?*

The stench of everlasting death was all around us, the black cords from each of those poor souls twisting and turning with each pulse, connecting into what looked like a black mountain in the centre of the chamber. It was like black, living worms, writhing and throbbing, sucking death in and out. Thousands and thousands of what used to be people, with hopes and dreams, lives and loved ones waiting forever to die. Moving from death to life and back again, but with no respite from the pain.

Looking around the room, I sensed my light beings moving away from me and I was left hanging in the air in the arms of my Guardian Angel. Her arms held me in safety, and her presence was as powerful and beautiful as it had been that evening in Angel's living room.

My ancestors and all the light beings in the room moved softly and silently through the air, each of them wrapping their arms and energies around each of the pulsating bodies. As they did so, their light dissolved the black cords piercing the hearts of those souls, and the cords fell down towards the mountain. I cried with pride as I saw the compassionate embrace from my ancestors holding each of those suffering corpses, releasing them one by one from their horrors. As they did so, it was as if they transferred some of their light to the darkness and the whole chamber shone brighter and lighter. The only sound left was that of the screaming dragons far beneath me. The walls were silent, but now lit up like the sun.

I turned my attention back to the ball of light – my grandmother, who radiated blue and white light around the dazzling chamber. I knew she couldn't have done anything else but follow her heart. It was in her blood to save these souls, as it was in mine.

The dragons flew higher and I saw the three of them clearly for the first time. They looked like those in fables and similar to the image in the stained glass window of the church. Their skin shining and wings beating furiously. Breathing fire, and flying around the cavern, I realised they were fighting. What

I had seen wasn't a mountain in the middle of the cave, but the back of a huge beast. Hundreds of feet tall, it gradually struggled to its feet, blood and gore dripping from its stinking teeth.

This was the drawing I'd seen in the book, but it wasn't a two-headed monster. This had three heads, two yellow-pointed horns on each, dripping with blood. It lashed out at the dragons, who continued to outsmart it, flying fast to remain out of the way of its claws as they ripped through the air. It roared and screamed in outrage as the dragons zoomed in and out of its reach, spitting fire as they swooped.

The beast suddenly seemed to notice that its thousands of prey were now free, and that the black cords were pulsing out what I could only assume was its own venom. It was pooling around the monster, and seemed to be tiring it. If this was how it had gained its strength, it was bound to be less powerful without it.

At that moment I heard what sounded like an explosion, and saw the whole side of the cavern drop away. Rocks and mud fell down on top of the monster, but the light bodies were unfazed and waited. There must have been a landslide outside, and now I was looking through the gap, up and out towards the quarry site. The full moon and stars lit up the cavern. It felt like days since we'd stood there sipping hot drinks and trying to stay warm. Instead, I was inside the hillside, held in the air by an angel and surrounded by light.

A wide dazzling beam of light appeared through the gap, filling the chamber with even more light until I was dazzled. It sparked and frazzled in a dynamic energetic column, and the light beings serenely and silently slipped onto it, each holding a broken soul as precious cargo, then disappeared from view. The light was too bright for me to look at, and it filled the cavern, burning brighter and brighter as each of my wonderful ancestors joined the procession of light upwards.

I heard another roar, and with one last effort the monster threw itself into the air, grabbing at the dragons, catching two of them and pulling them towards its stinking, rotten mouths. They screamed, yellow fire sparking out against its death hold. One in each hand, it started to crush them, and their screeches filled the air.

In answer to their pain, I saw the blue white light ball drop quickly towards the heart of the beast, as if to protect the dragons who had distracted the monster for as long as they could. It all happened so quickly, but it had the desired effect, and the monster let go of the dragons as its huge claws ripped through the air, screaming, roaring, filling the chamber with the sound of outrage. Released, the dragons escaped back to their cavern, their work done. I knew they'd be safe.

I screamed for my gran. I didn't know how things would work out, but I could not watch and let her sacrifice herself any more. Not for me, not for this town. Without thinking of what I was doing, I pulled myself from my Guardian Angel's grasp and felt myself drop quickly through the air towards the monster. It was my turn to protect my gran, to sacrifice myself for her. I fell hundreds of feet towards the monster, without fear or worry about what this would mean for me.

As if by magic, I managed to land in the middle of the monster's back, and grabbed tight to its stinking, oily hair. What I could do, I did not know. I was tiny, probably powerless, but I hoped that the distraction would give Gran enough time to get away if she wanted. But it was too greasy, and as the monster bucked and screamed, grasping towards the ball of light, my hands slipped. One of its huge stinking heads turned towards me, like I was a flea on a dog. It knew what we were doing, we were sharing the data as if we were all wired into the same computer.

I looked into its gigantic jaws of putrifying death and it was as if everything slowed down. The sounds, the smells, the darkness and the light, all slowed and stopped. We were all frozen in time. With a final shake, it threw me off and I felt myself slowly fall backwards. As I did so, I saw the column of light expand even more and reach the monster, then it too rose up in the beam and disappeared from view. I realised that everything was able to return to light, nothing was evil or terrible enough that it couldn't be redeemed. The chamber was almost empty.

I had a sensation of floating, a feeling of peace, my hands reaching up towards my family, my gran's face smiling, my mum, my ancestors all smiling at me as I fell.

27

When I opened my eyes, I was sitting on the stones beside my gran's grave. I could hear sirens in the distance and saw blue flashing lights racing on the road towards the quarry. Sleet hit me in the face making me blink, and I saw and heard Angel and Grizelle running towards me, calling my name. I was out. I was safe and free. I flexed my hands and stretched my body; everything felt fine. All my scratches and scrapes had disappeared, although my clothes were damp and ripped. Another bit of magic. I was out of the cavern and it didn't surprise me at all. I felt good, satisfied, energised and peaceful inside.

'How did you know I'd be here?' I croaked, then added, 'Sorry. Stupid question.' And they both laughed.

'We came straight here,' said Angel. 'As soon as that door closed on you, we knew we could find you here.'

'You came straight here? How is that possible? I thought I was away for hours. It certainly felt like it. Do you know what happened? I felt you were both there.'

'We were,' Grizelle said.

'And we weren't!' laughed Angel.

Grizelle began to explain something about how perception of time is always relative, but I didn't fully grasp what she said. I was just so relieved to be with them both again in the cold night air.

'The fire engines and police are off to the quarry. You'll know there's been a landside,' Angel told me. 'I think that's the last we'll hear of any further expansion at the quarry. Kirsten, and of course, her granddaughter, did well.'

I smiled and hugged them. These two ladies had been an amazing help to me since I arrived. And now I knew and could feel that I had lots more support. That felt good. I had a vision of Gran smiling at me, and I knew she wasn't far away. For the first time ever, I got that.

We linked arms and left Gran's grave behind, crossed the road, and walked back to Angel's flat in silence. We didn't need to say a word. We had all witnessed something amazing, but something I personally didn't have any words for. Grizelle hugged us both and went home. She looked tired but happy. We could hear the sirens of more emergency vehicles racing out to the quarry, but I knew it would be fine. No further work needed and the Stones would be safe. Gran's work was concluded.

Upstairs, Angel quickly lit the fire and prepared some hot drinks and cakes for us, and we sat silently in front of the flames, both lost in our own worlds for a while.

At the edge of my consciousness, there were was something that had been bothering me about the experience.

'Angel,' I asked. 'You know how you and Grizelle were in the chamber with me. Did you feel it?'

'We both did, Kirsty. We did a walking meditation, holding you surrounded by love. We knew you'd be fine. It's in your blood, after all!'

I relaxed back into the comfortable cushions and sipped my tea. 'My gran was really special in the whole experience, as you can imagine,' I told her. 'My mum and my other grand-parents were there. Even though they died before I was born, I recognised them and they were all behind me, with lots of other relatives and ancestors. It was incredible really, to feel all that power and strength and love.'

I hesitated for a few moments. 'There was one thing that was strange, though.' I looked nervously at her, wondering if she had already guessed. 'There was a man. It was my dad. He was there, but rather than stand behind me like the rest of my ancestors, he was off to the side, like you and Grizelle. What do you think that means?'

'What do you think it means?' she replied quietly.

'I'm not sure, but if he was with you and Grizelle, then I'm thinking that it's because he's not dead. Is that a crazy idea? But he *was* there. Grizelle said something about him being from an old Celtic family, like mine. Is that why he was there. Does he do stuff like Gran?'

'I really don't know, Kirsty.' She shrugged her shoulders. 'I'm sorry I can't help. Why don't you ask Grizelle?' She looked at me closely, as if she was going to say something else but changed her mind.

We agreed to talk more the next day when Grizelle was with us, but for now I needed to get to bed. I was exhausted from the whole experience.

For the first time ever I was asleep as soon as my head touched the pillow. There were no nightmares, no dreams, and no church bells to wake me.

I slept until ten o'clock the next morning, and woke to a beautiful cold but sunny day. Like the kind of winter days I remembered from my childhood. No fog, no rain, just blue sky and a topping of snow sitting on the far hills.

I felt bright and peaceful. I knew my family were all around me, and that made me feel loved and supported. It didn't matter that I couldn't see them physically. The feelings were there just the same. I realised in a way that it was simpler because they knew how much I loved them too.

I checked my phone and there were texts from London. What was I doing? When was I coming back? I knew then that I wouldn't be. I didn't want to be in London. It was time I made a life with some fun in it. I'd carried the ghosts of my childhood for too long, and there was no need anymore.

I replied to my friends, sent a quick email of resignation to work, and then decided not to bother replying to Derek. He didn't deserve my attention. He'd made his choices and so had I. My future didn't include him.

I quickly dressed and ran downstairs. I felt like I was bursting with energy. *Angel's Cakes* was full. People were chatting and animatedly talking about the protest and the quarry collapse. From the conversations I overheard, the council had announced an enquiry into the granting of planning permission, and decided that no further expansion would ever be permitted as the ground was so unsafe.

Delighted, I managed to squeeze into a recently vacated seat at the window, close to the angel displays. It felt Gran and Mum close by, and when I looked in the steamy reflection it was as if I was sitting in the middle of a big group of people. I know it was probably a trick of the light, but it made me smile.

Angel popped over with some mugs of coffee and hot buttered toast, and settled down with me for a brief break.

'What do you plan to do now?' she asked with an encouraging smile. 'I'm sort of feeling that you won't go back to London, will you?'

I laughed. 'It's hard to describe but I feel that I want a simpler life, you know? I'm finished with pointless paper-shuffling. I feel it's time I did something for me. Maybe something creative, I don't know. I'm sure something will turn up, and I get the feeling that I've not to worry about it.'

I sighed. 'For such a long time, I've felt as if I wasn't happy. Just like you were saying about when you were married. I wasn't unhappy but I knew I could be happier. I know I'm the kind of person who fills her mind with work so that I don't have to look at what I really want. So I think I should take some time out. Is it too trite to say I want to "find myself"?' She shook her head, her bright eyes shining back at me.

'Last night showed me that I can do anything, and that I am always loved and supported,' I told her. 'So that's good enough for me for now. I also realised something that might sound a bit daft. I realised that I take life too seriously. I don't let enough fun in, and yet I was missing out on the important stuff, you know?'

'I understand,' she said. 'For me, it's about letting things happen rather than feeling that I have to control everything, which is the way I used to be. If you try to control things, there can only ever be one outcome. When you let things go a bit, there is space for other possibilities to happen. And do you know what? It's less stressful. That's what I found and that's the life I like. Somehow, though, I have the feeling that you won't be sitting around for long'

The café door open and Grizelle strode in. She spotted us near the window and she stooped to give us both a hug.

'I'm so proud of you,' she whispered in my ear, 'and your gran and all your family are, too.'

I smiled back as she released me then sat down at the table. Her words were good to hear and I felt my family somewhere close, drawing in around me, comforting me. I remembered something Angel had once mentioned about honouring ourselves, and I knew that was what was really important to me. It was as if the whole experience had altered my core beliefs about myself. As if I had returned to the person I had been a long time ago, the one who had sat hidden inside me somewhere.

The life I had been leading was not honouring me. I wanted to lead a more simple life; one that was more fundamentally close to who I really am.

As we chatted quietly, surrounded by relieved, happy people, a group of the environmentalists arrived. Several of the customers cheered as they were spotted, and a few people went over to shake their hands, thanking them for all their efforts at the quarry.

Maggie was wearing a bright bandana to cover her hair. She looked pale, but smiled at everyone as she waited near the door. Sally caught sight of us and popped over to give Angel a brief hug. She assured us that Maggie was fine, the cut had looked worse than it was. They were delighted that the quarry expansion had been cancelled, so they were returning to the peace camp at Faslane, further up the river, and had come to say goodbye.

We wished them all well and they headed off alongside Grizelle, who had to get back to the shop.

The café was still fairly busy, and I noticed a number of people looking through the angel shop area. Sunbeams picked up a large picture of Archangel Gabriel and it shimmered in the light, as though it was something significant, a message of some kind.

As I sat wondering what it could be, one of Angel's staff came over and told me that there was a phone call for me.

'Are you sure?' I was surprised that anyone knew to reach me here.

'He asked if you were here,' the young girl replied. 'He's hanging on. The phone is through the back... just go through.'

'Who is it, Angel? Who could possibly be calling me here?' It must have been someone from the town. No-one else would have known that I'd be here with Angel.

I got up and walked slowly across the shop then squeezed in behind the counter to go into the back kitchen area. I had a really odd feeling again, like everything had slowed down. As I looked around at the shelves filled with food, ovens, the dishwasher, I couldn't seem to clear my head. It was like there was someone else there.

I picked up the receiver. I was feeling separate again from everything. Who could be calling me?

'Hello… Kirsty… is that you?'

A voice across twenty-five years. Instantly recognisable. I felt my breath catch in my throat. I tightened my grip on the receiver, holding it closer to my ear. 'Yes?'

'It's Dad, Kirsty. I'm at Newgrange in Ireland. The Stones have been moved. Kirsty, I need your help…'

THE END OF THE THIRTEEN STONES

Now turn over to read a preview of the next novel in the series

The Chamber Within

K.T Finegan

1

The sound of silent anticipation filled the old stone chamber as I stood with a hundred other souls. All of us lost in excitement, awaiting the winter solstice sun to appear through a tiny hole in the wall and fill the cavern with dawn light. The way it had for over five thousand years. It was as if I could hear my ancestors whispering in my ear. This was the right place for me. This felt like home.

We stood in reverence to the power of the sun and the ingenuity of Stone Age people, who had built this amazing place by hand from rock and soil, perfectly aligned with their vision of the winter sky. We waited, cameras and tablets ready to catch the magic moment of light in this temple to the sun, in deepest Ireland.

We waited. Someone official, perhaps from the tourist organisation who managed the ancient site, finally counted down to the dawn majesty and we stood ready as silent witnesses. Standing in the darkness towards the back of the monument, I couldn't see a thing. Faintly from outside, I could hear a dull drum beat. Hundreds of people stood there, unable to get inside but, like us, ready to welcome the dawn, and the new year. The shortest day; from now on, more sunlight. Like our ancient ancestors we, too, wanted to see the end of the winter.

The drums reached a pounding rhythmic crescendo, and then there was nothing but an unexpected, unnerving, deathly silence.

There's always that moment when you just know that something isn't right. You can hear it unsaid, an energy, an awareness that grips people. Nothing happened. No sunlight lit the chamber. Some people shuffled, some coughed, no-one spoke. No-one wanted to be the first to spoil the moment, to break the spell that had surrounded us. The special ones. Twenty-first century mystical believers, standing where our forefathers had stood, celebrating the sun.

And then it happened. Panic. No-one knew what to do. Pushing, pulling, running in the darkness. Hitting the sharp, rugged stones of the cave. Shouting, trying to reach loved ones. Fear. Screaming. Fuelling more panic. Not knowing where to go, and all thoughts of specialness gone. Instead, primeval survival; perhaps we were closer to our Stone Age ancestors than we had realised.

The crowd ran around as a wild group, hunting for the hidden exit then bending down almost double to crawl back along the tight, low passageway outside the monument. In haste to get away, and yet not knowing what awaited them.

But for some reason they couldn't see me. It was as if I was invisible. And as they all turned to run, screaming in panic that the sun hadn't come up, I was knocked off my feet and fell to the floor. My face forced into the cold, dank ground, I could taste its bitterness. I couldn't shout out with earth in my mouth and nose. I felt the pain of winter boots on my back and head, treading me into the floor of the cavern. Standing on me, kicking me, bruising me, and I felt myself faint. Dropping into a darkness, a rushing pulse in my ears, pain in my body. I felt myself give up. Give in. No oxygen, my nose and mouth filling with soil. I was dying.

*

I sat up, panting for breath, in the cold, dark air of my child-hood bedroom, and it took me a moment to realise I was safe. None of it was real. No-one was standing on me. I was in bed, not in a darkened cave. Slowly, my breathing returned to normal. Sweat had rolled down my neck; my damp hair icy in the pre-dawn chill.

I sat up quickly, then forced myself out of bed with a shud-der. Stumbling about in the dark, not really sure where I was. It was another nightmare. The same one I'd had for the last few nights. It had been such an unsettling time. Since my father, who I hadn't seen for over twenty years, had called to ask for my help.

Newgrange. A place I had only recently heard of. An ancient stone chamber in Ireland, built as a temple to the winter sun, and one that my father seemed to think was in danger of some kind. And here we were, a week or so before the winter solstice celebration, and I was having nightmares about it.

In the predawn haze of a Scottish winter, I felt for my thick, fleecy dressing gown, rammed my feet into sheepskin slip-pers, and then pulled a tartan, woollen blanket around my shoulders, before heading downstairs to the relative warmth of the kitchen stove.

I used my sleeve to open up the still-warm metal handle and threw in some firelighters, thin twigs for kindling, and a couple of logs. Closing the glass door again quickly, I knew it would catch light and soon warm the old cottage. Within a few minutes, I had made some tea and sat huddled against the fireplace.

Flames crackled, logs spat and hissed, and silent shad-ows danced around the room. Outside, the winter storm had relaxed slightly. Thick snow and high winds had been my only visitors for days, and I was finding the prolonged isola-tion unsettling.

Sitting in my late gran's cottage – left to me as her only living relative – I felt her all around me. Almost like a breath somewhere near my ear. I sensed her moving close as if to comfort me. I sat back against the cushions, closed my eyes, and surrendered towards sleep. It was the space where I felt closest to all those I had lost.

About The Author

KT Finegan lives in her home city of Glasgow where she writes, and offers workshops and intuitive coaching. Please visit www.ktfinegan.com for further information.

Lightning Source UK Ltd.
Milton Keynes UK
UKOW06f0234270716

279330UK00008B/59/P